Dear Reader

We're constantly striving to bring you the best romance fiction by the most exciting authors, and in Tender Romance™ we're especially keen to feature fresh, sparkling, emotionally exhilarating novels! Modern love stories to suit your every mood: poignant, deeply moving stories; lively, upbeat romances with sparks flying; or sophisticated, edgy novels with a cosmopolitan flavour.

All our authors are special, and we hope you continue to enjoy each month's new selection of Tender Romances. This month we're delighted to feature another novel with extra fizz! In Liz Fielding's fast-paced, witty novel meet Philly and laugh along with her (and at her!) as she attempts to become a city girl in London…

We hope you enjoy this book by Liz Fielding—it's fresh, flirty and feel-good!—and look out for future sparkling stories in Tender Romance™. If you'd like to share your thoughts and comments with us, do please write to:

The Tender Romance Editors
Harlequin Mills & Boon Ltd
Eton house, 18-24 Paradise Road
Richmond
Surrey TW9 1SR
Or email us at: tango@hmb.co.uk

Happy reading!

The Editors

Liz Fielding started writing at the age of twelve, when she won a writing competition at school. After that early success there was quite a gap—during which she was busy working in Africa and the Middle East, getting married and having children—before her first book was published in 1992. Now readers worldwide fall in love with her irresistible heroes and adore her independent-minded heroines.

Visit Liz's website for news and extracts of upcoming books at www.lizfielding.com

In 2001 Liz Fielding won the prestigious RITA® award from Romance Writers of America for THE BEST MAN AND THE BRIDESMAID!

Recent titles by the same author:

A PERFECT PROPOSAL
  (in 2-in-1 *The Engagement Effect* with Betty Neels)
THE CORPORATE BRIDEGROOM•
THE MARRIAGE MERGER•
THE TYCOON'S TAKEOVER•

Boardroom Bridegrooms trilogy

CITY GIRL IN TRAINING

BY
LIZ FIELDING

All the characters in this book have no existence outside the imagination of the author, and have no relation whatsoever to anyone bearing the same name or names. They are not even distantly inspired by any individual known or unknown to the author, and all the incidents are pure invention.

First published in Great Britain 2002
Harlequin Mills & Boon Limited,
Eton House, 18-24 Paradise Road, Richmond, Surrey TW9 1SR

© Liz Fielding 2002

ISBN 0 263 83048 9

Set in Times Roman 10½ on 12½ pt.
02-1202-42830

Printed and bound in Spain
by Litografía Rosés, S.A., Barcelona

CHAPTER ONE

The house is on fire and you only have time to grab one item of clothing. Would you choose:
a. the kickin' hot purple leather miniskirt that turns heads in the street?
b. your expensive go-anywhere black suit?
c. a pair of washed-thin jogging pants that you were wearing when you first met the man of your dreams?
d. the designer skirt you bought in a sale? You'll never get a bargain like that again.
e. the sweater knitted for you by your grand-mother?

'ARE you sure you don't want to take this sweater, Philly? Aunt Alice will expect to see you wearing it at Christmas…' My mother looked up when I didn't answer and caught me looking at the quiz in the magazine she'd bought me on her last-minute dash to the shops. 'Save that for the journey, dear,' she said, as if I were six years old, instead of nearly twenty-three, 'or you won't have anything to read on the train.'

I heroically resisted the urge to tell her that while I was the baby of the family, the one who didn't get a starred first at university, I was quite capable of buying myself a magazine, and instead gave her my full attention. Her question, however, had been purely rhetorical. She'd already unzipped the corner of my case and tucked away the sweater.

It figured.

I'd been haunted by that sweater ever since my Great-Aunt Alice had knitted it for me. It was pale blue and fluffy and I loathed it. I'd planned on putting it in a carton of clothes to be stored in the attic, hoping that a moth would consider it a suitable home for her offspring.

'You really should have bought a new case. I'm not at all happy about this zip.'

'The zip is fine,' I said. At least it had been fine until my mother had added that sweater. 'I'm catching a train to London, not flying to the other side of the world.' Unlike my parents who were abandoning me, throwing me upon the mercy of strangers while they went on a world tour visiting their far-flung offspring.

My father had taken early retirement and it was, my mother had told me, time for them to have a little fun visiting my three clever and adventurous brothers in New Zealand, California and South Africa, respectively. And my beautiful, and equally adventurous, clever married sister, and her new babies, in Australia.

Fun! They were *parents*. Parents weren't supposed to have fun. They were supposed to stay home, do the crossword, play Scrabble and drink cocoa and I told them so.

They thought that was very funny.

I WASN'T JOKING!

But then, neither were they. They'd spent the last thirty-five years bringing up their family and now they were seriously intent on enjoying themselves. I was the only fly in the ointment. Twenty-two years old, still living at home. Still dating the boy next door. With no sign of a wedding any time soon.

Worse was to come.

I'd assumed they'd go on their extended holiday happy in the knowledge that I'd be there to take care of things while they were away. And the up side was that, with the house to myself, I'd have a real opportunity to move things along with Don. Get his mind out from under the bonnet of his car, away from his mother, and inject some physicality into our relationship.

I was getting desperate for some action while I was still young enough to enjoy it.

But my father's successor had been looking for somewhere to rent while he and his family found a house in the district. The deal had been done before I'd even heard about it. I'd appealed to my mother, but she'd said it was nothing to do with her. And then—and here was an extraordinary coincidence— my boss (the one who played golf with my dad every Sunday morning) asked me if I'd consider a six-month secondment to the City. Working in a merchant bank. Honing my skills for the next step up the ladder. Promotion. Something I'd been avoiding for the last two years. Promotion meant moving.

But Maybridge was alive with the twanging of strings being pulled and, before I'd known it, my

mother had been on the old girls' network, finding me
somewhere to live.

'It'll do you good to have a change of scene,' she
said, over my protests. 'You're stuck in a rut in
Maybridge. Gone as far as you can at the local branch
of the bank…' Everything came in threes, and apparently ruts were no exception. 'And Don takes you for
granted. It will do you both good to stand back and
look at where you're going.'

I knew where I was going—I'd known since I was
ten years old—but my mother had a look about her
that warned me that any argument would be a waste
of breath. An I-know-what's-best-for-you look. An
unexpectedly knowing look that suggested a little en-
forced separation might shake Don into action.

Nearly twenty-three years old and still a virgin, I
was getting desperate for some action.

All this talk of ruts was, however, a bit hard to take
from a woman who'd lived with the same man, in the
same house, for nearly forty years.

Not that I was criticising her for that. It was what
I wanted, too. A lifetime with one man, in one house,
raising a family. Just like my mother.

And Don wanted the same thing. Well, obviously
he didn't want a *man*, he wanted me, he'd said so.
He just wasn't doing anything about making it happen. Perhaps my imminent departure would jolt him
out of his complacency.

I'd found him in his garage working on the small
vintage car he'd been restoring for what seemed like
for ever, told him my news and held my breath.

'London?' he said, with that sweet, puzzled expression that made him look as innocent as a baby. Okay, he was innocent. And sweet. If he'd been anything else, I'd have been beating off other girls since he was old enough to shave. But he'd only ever had eyes for me. He pushed back his floppy blond fringe, leaving a smear of grease on his forehead, to look at me with concern. 'What on earth will you do in London?'

No, no, no!

He was supposed to leap to his feet, wrap me in his arms and tell me that I wasn't going anywhere without him.

'Going for the promotion that's due to me,' I said, irrationally irritable. 'Seeing the sights. Having some fun,' I added, hoping to provoke a little possessiveness.

Why would he be possessive when I'd only ever had eyes for him?

Don frowned but not, apparently, at the thought of me having fun. 'You mean you're going for good?' For one heart-stopping moment I thought I'd got through to him. That he'd finally realised that, unless he did something about it, I wouldn't be around to read his mind and put the right spanner in his hand whenever he needed it.

My imagination ran momentarily wild with anticipation that he'd leap to his feet, wrap me...etc., etc.

'Yes,' I said. That wasn't quite true, but if I were promoted I would have to move to a larger branch somewhere else. I should have done it a long time ago, but I was comfortable in my rut. Unlike my siblings, I didn't have an adventurous bone in my body. I'd flown once and I'd been so frightened I'd been sick. Nothing would induce me to repeat the experience. Besides, I liked living at home. Next door to the boy next door.

'But you've been working there since you left college,' Don said.

His concern about me moving on from my present job was wearing a bit thin. He was supposed to be shocked that I was leaving *him*.

'Maybe it's time to move on,' I said. And waited for him to do something to change my mind. Exclamations of heartbreak would be a start. Followed by a suggestion that we catch the next plane to Bali and get married right away. On a beach. In the moonlight.

Bali? What was I thinking of? I didn't want to go to Bali. That would mean getting on a plane. Two planes if I wanted to come home.

All this talk of travelling must have gone to my head.

I needn't have worried, however, because he did none of the above. Just did that thing with his fringe again, looking adorably helpless, so that I wanted to kiss him and tell him that I didn't mean it. That I wasn't going anywhere. I just about managed to restrain myself. 'Oh, well, I suppose I should say congratulations.' Then, 'I'll really miss you.' That was marginally better, but my smile was a fraction too fast. 'I'll have more time to work on the car, though.'

Er, when? He already spent every spare moment cherishing tender loving care on its engine, bodywork, upholstery, when it was my bodywork that was crying out for a little of that TLC.

'Great,' I said. But through gritted teeth.

'London?' He repeated the word as if it were a strange and mythical place instead of a sprawling city a scant hour from Maybridge by train. 'I'm sure you'll have a terrific time.'

BUT I DON'T WANT TO GO!

My scream of frustration was silent, however. A girl had her pride.

But why couldn't he see that I wasn't looking for a terrific time? That what I wanted was for him to tell me to forget all about London, suggest I move in with him and his widowed mother while we looked for a flat we could share…

I didn't bother to ask any of these questions out loud. I already knew the answer.

Mrs Cooper, a vapid hypochondriac who'd never recovered from the fact that her husband had decamped with his secretary, was always very sweet to my face. I had a strong suspicion, however, that beneath the saccharine exterior she hated me playing with Don just as much now as when he'd been a clever twelve-year-old and I'd distracted him from his homework. There was no way she'd want me so dangerously close to her precious son.

I was seriously tempted to strip off and seduce him, right there and then in the garage, just to spite her. But the floor was bare concrete, the temperature freez-

ing and Don's hands were covered with motor oil.
Only an idiot—or a desperate woman—would remove
her thermals under such unpromising circumstances.
Okay, so I was desperate, but, short of experience as
I was, I suspected that, shivering and blue with cold,
I wasn't going to light anyone's fire.

'I do rather envy you, to be honest,' Don said, dis-
tracting me with an odd hint of longing in his voice.
'All those museums…'

Museums? That was his idea of a terrific time?
Sweet, trusting soul that he was, I could have hugged
him. But his overalls were covered in oil, too. Of
course if I'd been wearing that fluffy sweater I'd have
made the sacrifice.

'Actually,' he said, with more animation than he'd
shown all evening, 'when you go to the Science
Museum you might take a look at…'

The Science Museum? He thought my idea of a
fantastic time was an afternoon at the Science
Museum? I might take a turn around the V&A to look
at the jewellery and fashions but…

'Promise?' he said.

Promise? Promise what? Oh, heck, I should have
been listening. 'Why don't you come up and spend
the weekend with me?' I suggested, suddenly seeing
the possibilities… 'We could go together.'

He looked slightly uncomfortable and, concentrat-
ing on wiping his hands on a rag, he said, 'I don't
think I could leave Mother on her own overnight. She
suffers so with her nerves.'

So she did.

She managed to get through the day well enough, while he was at work. She saved up her attacks to coincide with any plans I had for Don. Which was why, on Friday, having waved my parents off on their great adventure, I had to haul my own case aboard the London train. He'd taken the afternoon off to drive me to the station, but his mother had had one of her 'little turns' just before we'd been due to leave.

I'd considered having a turn of my own. Flinging myself on the floor and drumming my heels on the hall carpet. But Don had looked so miserable that I'd told him to go back to his mother and wait for the doctor, while I called a taxi and put myself on the train.

As Maybridge disappeared into the icy rain of a November afternoon I settled down with a cheese and pickle sandwich and a comfortingly large hot chocolate drink and, since I had an hour to fill, I took out the magazine.

'Are You a Tiger or a Kitten?' screamed at me from a cover flash. I didn't need a quiz to answer that one. I was nearly twenty-three years old, I had a mother who was still treating me like a child and a boyfriend who'd apparently mislaid his libido.

I was a kitten, right?

Wrong.

Having worked my way through the multiple-choice questions, I discovered that I'd been wildly optimistic.

I was a mouse. Or maybe an ostrich.

That, according to the quiz, was why I was sitting

on a train for London when I wanted to stay in Maybridge.

That was why my boyfriend put his mother first. (And because he was sweet and kind and she was a manipulative old witch.) Why I was going to spend Christmas pulling crackers with Great-Aunt Alice instead of getting pulled by Don.

I was too easygoing. Too undemanding. My expectations were so low, they barely registered. I picked up my cheese sandwich and then put it down again quickly. Cheese. A mouse *would* choose a cheese sandwich.

I should have chosen the fashionable roast vegetables in sun dried tomato bread. But, mouse that I was, I *loved* cheese.

I should be wearing designer label jeans with high heels, instead of an old pair that had once belonged to the last of my brothers to leave home—shortened to fit my pathetically short legs—with a pair of cheap trainers I'd bought from the market. (I was saving up to get married, okay?)

I should have my nails professionally manicured. I should at least have painted them with something more exciting than the pale pink nail polish I'd borrowed from my mother.

I might never have wanted to be a tiger, but surely I should at least aspire to be a kitten?

Unfortunately any attempt to change my character would only raise a patronising smile in Maybridge. I'd lived there all my life. Who would take me seriously if I changed into a scarlet-nailed temptress overnight?

But it occurred to me that in London, where no one knew me, I could be whatever I chose. I had to face facts. Being mouse-like, I hadn't been able to untie Don from his mother's apron strings and fix him to mine.

Maybe my mother—tough though it was to admit this—was right. Maybe a break would do us both good. Don had six months to experience life without me at his side to hand him a wrench before he'd even asked for it.

And I had six months to put on some gloss, put an edge on my character, so that when I went back to Maybridge Don would be down that aisle before he— or his mother—knew what had hit him.

As the train arrived in Paddington I stuffed the magazine into my shoulder bag for further study and grabbed my bulging suitcase from the rack.

New job. New life. New clothes. I was in London and I was going to make the most of it.

I didn't actually growl as I joined the crowds heading for the underground, but I was beginning to take to the idea of being a tiger.

CHAPTER TWO

It's the rush hour and raining. You hail the same taxi as a tall, dark and handsome stranger and he suggests sharing. Do you:
a. think it's your birthday, flirt like mad until you reach your destination, then as you leave the cab hand him your phone number with a look that says 'Call me…'?
b. remind yourself that your mother would not approve, but it is raining and he doesn't look like a serial killer. What could be the harm?
c. tell him to get lost and leave him standing on the pavement?
d. let him take the taxi and wait for another one?
e. walk?

HAVING battled with the intricacies of the underground system, only going in the wrong direction twice, I finally emerged into the light of day. When I say light of day, I'm using poetic licence. What actually confronted me was the dark of a wet November evening.

And when I say wet, I do mean wet. No poet needed. The rain, miserable icy drizzle that had perfectly matched my mood when I'd left home, had intensified to the consistency of stair-rods.

16

In the country it would have been quite dark. But this was London where the neon never set; excitingly opulent shop windows and the rainbow colours of a million Christmas lights were reflected in the wet street, cutting through the gathering gloom.

And there were people, hundreds and hundreds of people, all with somewhere to go and in a hurry to get there.

I stood in the entrance to the underground, *A-Z* in hand, trying to orientate myself as impatient travellers pushed past me. On paper, it didn't seem far to Sophie and Kate Harrington's flat, but I was well aware that distance, on paper, could be deceiving. And my problems with north and south on the underground system had seriously undermined any confidence in my ability to map read. A taxi seemed like a wise investment and as I glanced up I spotted the yellow light on a cruising black cab.

I'd never hailed a taxi before—in Maybridge taxis didn't cruise for custom, you had to telephone for one—but I knew how to do it. In theory. I'd seen people do it on television often enough. You stood on the kerb, raised your hand and yelled 'Taxi!'...

I'd never make it to the kerb before it passed so I raised my hand and waved hopefully, but, realising that my self-consciously ladylike rendition of 'Taxi!' didn't stand a chance of being heard over the noise of traffic, I tried again, this time yelling loud enough to wake the dead. I didn't care. It had worked! The driver was heading for the kerb, pulling up a few yards ahead of me.

Wow! Who was the mouse now? I thought smugly as I grabbed the handle of my suitcase and, towing it after me, I cut recklessly through the crowds who were charging along, heads collectively down against the rain. Before I got to the kerb, however, someone had already opened the taxi door and was closing his umbrella prior to boarding.

'Hey, you! That's mine!' I declared, uncharacteristically tiger-like in my defence of my first London taxi, despite the fact that my adversary towered above me.

The black silk umbrella he was holding collapsed in a shower of rainwater, most of which went over me, and the taxi thief glanced at me with every indication of impatience.

'On the contrary, I hailed it before you even saw it,' he said, giving me the briefest of glances. Brief was apparently all it took. After a moment's astonished gaze, he muttered something beneath his breath that I didn't quite catch—but didn't for a moment believe was complimentary—and, with a look of resignation that suggested he was being a fool to himself, he stood back and gestured at the open door. 'Take it. Before you drown.'

Oh, no. This was bad. I could be mad at a man who nicked my cab, but I couldn't take it if it was rightfully his, even if my need was clearly the greater.

He did, after all, have an umbrella.

But I was already so wet that no amount of rain would make any difference. As I dithered on the kerb, he was rapidly getting the same way. But it had only taken a moment's reflection, a pause long enough for my brain to override my mouth, for me to realise that I had in fact seen him standing at the edge of the pavement in that moment when I'd looked up from the *A-Z*. That my own efforts to attract the driver's attention from the back of the pavement had gone unheeded. Feeling very stupid, the tiger in me morphed back into mouse.

'No, really,' I said. 'I'm sorry…'

'Oh, for heaven's sake.' He seized the handle of my suitcase, crammed with everything I might need for the next six months and weighing a ton, and tossed it into the cab without noticeable effort. 'Stop wittering and get in.'

'Would one of you get in?' the driver demanded testily. 'I've got a living to make.'

'Maybe we could share,' I said, scrambling in after my suitcase. My irritable knight errant paused in the act of closing the door behind me. 'I'm not going far and you could…um…we could…' He waited for me to finish. 'At least you'd be in the dry.'

Oh, heck. This wasn't like the quiz at all. I wasn't supposed to do the asking. But then the quiz wasn't real life.

In my real life I didn't offer to share taxis with tall, dark and handsome strangers. In my real life Friday evenings were spent handing Don his spanners as he talked endlessly about the intricacies of the internal combustion engine; a well-drilled theatre nurse to his mechanical surgeon. Comfortable. Familiar. Safe.

Nothing to get the heart racing. Not the way mine was racing now.

'Where are you going?'

I told him and he raised his brows a fraction.

'Is that on your way?' I asked.

After a moment's hesitation, he nodded, told the driver where to go, then climbed in and pulled down the jump seat opposite me, sitting sideways, his legs stretched across the width of the cab, so that his knees and feet wouldn't intrude on my space.

He had the biggest feet I'd ever seen and as I stared at them I found myself wondering if it was true about the size of a man's feet indicating the size of, well, other extremities...

'You're new in London aren't you?' he said, and I looked up. The corner of his mouth had kinked up in a knowing smile and I blushed, certain that he could read my mind.

'Just this minute arrived.' There was no point in pretending otherwise. I'd dressed for warmth and comfort rather than style. With nothing more glamorous than baby cream on my face—I'd chewed off my lipstick in the tussle with the underground—and my hair neon-red candyfloss from the damp, I was never going to pass as a sophisticated City-girl. 'I suppose the suitcase is a dead giveaway,' I said, wishing I'd taken a lot more trouble over my appearance.

A tiger, according to my magazine, would always leave the house prepared to meet the man of her dreams. But how often did *that* happen? Besides, I'd left the man of my dreams in Maybridge. Hadn't I?

'And the *A-Z*,' I added, stuffing it into my shoulder bag, alongside the treacherous magazine.

'Not the suitcase,' he replied. 'It was your willingness to surrender a taxi at this time of day that betrayed you. You won't do it twice.'

'I won't?'

'They're rarer than hen's teeth.'

Hen's teeth? 'Are they rare?' I asked, confused. It seemed unlikely. Hens weren't on any endangered list...

'I've never seen one.' Oh, *stocking tops*! The rain was dripping from my hair and trickling icily down the back of my neck. I suspected that it had seeped right into my brain. 'But then I've never felt any desire to look into a hen's beak,' he added.

'No one ever does,' I replied. 'Big mistake.' And he was kind enough to smile, giving me ample opportunity to see for myself that his own teeth left nothing to be desired.

In the dark and wet of the pavement I hadn't noticed much more than the fact that my 'tall, dark stranger' was the requisite 'tall'. Of course, when describing yourself as one point six metres was pure vanity, *everyone* seemed tall. But he was really, really tall. Several inches taller than Don, who was my personal yardstick for tall.

And his voice. I'd noticed that, too.

Low and gravelly, it was the voice of a man you just knew it wouldn't be wise to mess with. Yet his impatience was softened by velvet undertones. Sort of like Sean Connery, but without the Scottish accent.

Now I was sitting opposite him I could see that the 'dark' bit fitted him, too. I sat mesmerised as a drop of rainwater gathered and slid down the jet curve of an untidy curl before dropping into the turned-up collar of his overcoat. And I shivered.

Tall and dark. His skin so deeply tanned that he looked Italian, or possibly Greek.

But he struck out on handsome.

There was nothing smooth or playboy pretty about his features. His cheekbones were too prominent, his nose less than straight and there was a jagged scar just above his right eyebrow, giving the overall impression of a man who met life head-on and occasionally came off worst.

That was okay. There was something about a cliché that was so off-putting. Two out of three was just about right. Tall, dark and dangerous was more like it, because his eyes more than made up for any lack of symmetry. They were sea-green, deep enough to drown in and left me with the heart-racing impression that until now I might have been dreaming in sepia.

'Have you come far?' he asked, in an attempt to engage me in conversation. Presumably to stop me from staring.

I was jerked back to reality. 'Oh…um …no. Not really. From Maybridge. It's near…er…' I struggled for a coherent response. I was used to having to explain exactly where Maybridge was. People constantly confused it with Maidenhead, Maidstone and a dozen other towns that began with the same sound, but my mind refused to co-operate.

'I know where Maybridge is,' he said, rescuing me from my pitiful lapse of memory. 'I have friends who live in Upper Haughton.'

'Upper Haughton!' I exclaimed, clutching at geographical straws. Upper Haughton was a picture-perfect village a few miles outside Maybridge that had outgrown its agricultural past and was now the province of the seriously rich. 'Yes, that's it. It's near Upper Haughton.'

The mouse in me wanted to groan, bury my face in my hands. Wanted to go back five minutes so that I could keep my big mouth shut and let him steal my taxi. His taxi.

But the tiger in me wanted to write my name and telephone number on a card and murmur 'call me' in a sultry voice. Since he must by now believe I was at least one sandwich short of a picnic, it was perhaps fortunate that I didn't have a card handy and was thus saved the embarrassment of making a total fool of myself.

Instead, I glanced at my wrist-watch, not because I wanted to know the time—I had no pressing engagement—but to avoid looking into his eyes again.

'We're nearly there,' he said. Then, 'Are you staying long? In London.'

'Six months,' I said. 'My parents are travelling…Australia, South Africa, America…and they decided to let the house…' I was 'wittering' again and, remembering his impatience, stopped myself. 'So here I am.'

'While the cat's away?' he suggested, with another of those knowing smiles.

Clearly he hadn't had any trouble spotting that I was a mouse. Fortunately, the taxi swept up to the front of a stunningly beautiful riverside apartment building, terraced in sweeping lines and lit up like an ocean liner, and I was saved the necessity of answering him. For a moment I sat open-mouthed at the sight while, apparently impatient to be rid of me, my companion opened the door and stepped out, lifting my case onto the footpath. Then, gentleman that he was, he opened his umbrella and handed it to me as I followed him, before turning to speak to the driver while I dug out my purse and found a five pound note.

'Put that away,' he said as I offered it.

'No, really, I insist,' I said. I couldn't let him pay my fare. He didn't bother to argue. He just closed the taxi door, picked up my suitcase and headed for the front door, leaving me with a five pound note in one hand and his umbrella in the other. The taxi drove off.

'Hey, wait...' I wasn't sure whether I was shouting at the driver, who clearly hadn't realised he still had a fare, or Mr Tall, Dark and Dangerous himself.

I'd been warned about the security system on the front door. You had to have a smart card, or ring the bell of the person you were visiting so that they could let you into the building. TDD bypassed the system by catching the door as someone left the building, and was now holding it open. Standing in the entrance. Waiting for me to join him.

He wasn't going anywhere, I realised.

'While the cat's away…' he'd said.

And my memory instantly filled in the blank. 'The mouse will play.'

And I hadn't denied it.

Did he think I couldn't wait to get started? Expect to be invited in? Offered…and I swallowed hard…coffee? Had my invitation to share the taxi been completely misunderstood?

I realised just how rash I'd been. Naïve. Worse…just plain stupid.

I'd allowed this man whom I'd never met before, whose name I didn't even know, to give the driver the address. I hadn't heard what he'd said and, too late, it occurred to me that I could be anywhere.

And who'd miss me?

I'd actually told him that my parents were on the other side of the world, for heaven's sake!

How long would it be before Sophie and Kate Harrington raised the alarm when I didn't arrive? When I'd spoken to Sophie, she hadn't been exactly enthusiastic about me moving in. In fact I'd got the distinct impression that she, like me, had had her arm painfully twisted.

She certainly wouldn't be dialling the emergency services today. Or tomorrow. Not until Don called, anyway…

Anticipation of his agonised realisation that I might not even have got on the train, that my disappearance might be entirely his fault for not seeing me off, made me feel momentarily happier.

The pleasure was short-lived, however, swamped by instant recall of a lifetime of my mother's awful warnings about the inadvisability of taking lifts from strangers. And with that thought came relief.

My mother, even from thirty thousand feet, came to my rescue as, pushing the five-pound note into my jacket pocket, I gripped my attack alarm. It was just a small thing on a keyring and I'm ashamed to say that I'd laughed when she'd given it to me, made me promise I'd carry it with me while I was in London. But, as she'd pointed out, I'd need a new keyring so it might as well be this one…

I sent a belated—and silent—thank-you heavenward before forcing my mouth into an approximation of a smile and looking up at the man I'd decided was tall, dark and *dangerous*. As if that were a *good* thing.

'You really didn't have to see me right to the door,' I said, trying on a laugh for size. It wasn't convincing.

'I wouldn't,' he assured me, 'if I didn't live in the apartment next door to you.'

'Next door?' He lived in the same block? Next door? Relief surged through me and I very nearly laughed.

'Shall we get inside?' he said coolly. He'd clearly cottoned on to my unease and was offended. 'If you'll just close the umbrella—'

In my hurry to comply, I yanked my hand out of my pocket and the keyring alarm flew out with it.

I made a wild grab for it and as my fingers closed over it I felt the tiny switch shift. I said one heartfelt word. Fortunately, it was obliterated by a banshee wail that my mother probably heard halfway to Australia.

Startled by the blast of sound, I let go of the umbrella, which, caught by a gust of wind, bowled away across the entrance and towards the road. TDD—his patience tried beyond endurance—swore briefly and let my suitcase drop as he lunged after it. It was too much for the over-stressed zip and the case burst open in a shower of underwear. Plain, white, *comfortable* underwear. The kind you'd never admit to wearing. He froze, transfixed by the horror of the moment, and the world seemed to stand still, catch its breath.

Then reality rushed back in full colour. With surround sound.

The rain, the piercing, mind-deadening noise of the alarm, the red-hot embarrassment that was right off any scale yet invented.

I was gripping the keyring in my fist, as if I could somehow contain the noise. There was a trick to switching it off—otherwise any attacker could do it. But I was beyond rational thought.

TDD's mouth was moving, but I couldn't hear what he was saying and finally he grabbed my wrist, prised open my fingers and dropped the wretched thing on the footpath. Then he put his heel on it and ground it flat. It seemed to take for ever before the sound finally died.

The silence, if anything, was worse.

'Thank you,' I said when the feeling came back to my ears, but my voice came out as little more than a squeak. A mouse squeak and heaven alone knew that at that moment I wished I were a real mouse—one with a hole to disappear down.

'Wait here,' he said, and the chill factor in his voice turned the gravel into crushed ice. Well, it wouldn't take a genius to work out why I was holding an attack alarm. He'd surrendered his taxi to me, refused my share of the fare, and I'd reacted to his kindness as if he were some kind of monster.

As my abused knight errant disappeared into the darkness in search of his umbrella, I knew that I should go after him, help him track it down. I told myself he'd probably prefer it if I didn't. That was what the 'wait here' had been all about. A keep-your-distance-before-you-do-any-more-damage command. Besides, I could hardly leave my knickers scattered across the entrance to this unbelievably grand block of flats.

I captured a pair that was about to blow away and stuffed it into my pocket. I knew I should wait for his return, apologise abjectly, offer to pay for any repairs. After all that wasn't any old cheap-and-cheerful bumbershoot. The kind that it didn't matter much if you left it on the bus. The kind I regularly left on buses.

Gathering the rest of my scattered belongings, I reasoned that waiting was not necessary. He lived next door. I could put a note through his letterbox later. I sincerely believed that when he'd had a moment to think, calm down, he'd prefer that.

Which was why I stuffed my clothes back into the case as fast as I could before sprinting for the lift.

*   *   *

Sophie Harrington took her time about opening the door. I stood there with my case gripped under both my arms to prevent the contents falling out, wishing she'd hurry up.

I'd promised myself while I'd been travelling up in the lift that next time I met my new next-door neighbour I'd be dressed tidily, with my hair and my mouth under control. I didn't expect him to be impressed, but hoped he'd realise I wasn't the complete idiot he'd—with good reason—thought me.

Heck, even I thought I was an idiot. And I knew better.

But if Sophie didn't hurry up, I'd still be standing in the hall when he reached the top floor.

It wasn't an appealing prospect and I hitched up my suitcase and rang the bell again. The door was instantly flung open by a girl in a bathrobe and a bad mood.

Oh, good start.

Having gravely offended the next door neighbour, I'd now got my new flatmate out of the shower.

And if I hadn't already known just how bad I looked—the lift had mirrored walls—her expression would have left me in no doubt.

'You must be Philly Gresham,' she said, with a heaven-help-us sigh. 'I'm Sophie Harrington. You'd better come in.'

'Thanks.' I stepped into the hall, still clinging to my suitcase and unwilling to put it down. The floor was pale polished hardwood and I didn't want to make a mess. 'I've had a bit of an accident,' I said, unnecessarily. But I felt someone had to fill that huge, unwelcoming silence. 'The zip broke.'

Sophie's older sister, Kate, appeared behind her and, taking one look at me, said, 'Good grief, did you swim here?' Then, kinder, she said, 'I'll show you your room. You can dump that and have a hot shower while Sophie makes a pot of tea. You look as if you could do with a cup.'

That had to be the understatement of the year.

Sophie didn't look as if making a pot of tea had been part of her immediate plans, but after another sigh—just to reinforce the message—she flounced off.

'Take no notice of my little sister,' Kate said as she led the way. 'She had other plans for your room. She'll get over it.'

'Oh?' I said politely, imagining a study, or a work-room.

'There's a stunning new man at work. He's just moved down from Aberdeen and he's looking for somewhere to live. She'd planned to seduce him with low-rent accommodation.' She glanced back at me, her expression solemn, but her eyes danced with hu-mour. 'A mistake, don't you think? Suppose he moved in and then brought home a succession of equally stunning girls?'

'Nothing but trouble,' I agreed, with equal solem-nity.

We exchanged a look that suggested that, two years older than Sophie, we were both too old, too wise to ever do anything that stupid and I decided that, while the jury was out on Sophie, I was going to like Kate.

'I was quite relieved when Aunt Cora phoned and asked if we could put you up, to be honest. Sophie threw a tantrum but she knows that when Aunt Cora commands…' She obviously thought I knew what she was talking about.

'Aunt Cora?'

'My mother's sister. This is her flat. A small part of the spoils of a very lucrative divorce settlement. Happily she prefers to live in France so we get to house-sit.'

'At a price.'

'We just pay the expenses, which admittedly are not low…' Then, 'Oh, you mean *you*.' And she laughed. 'Don't worry about it. Sophie'll come round.' She stopped. 'This is your room.'

And she opened a door to the kind of bedroom I'd only ever seen in lifestyle articles in the Sunday supplements. A blond wood floor, taupe walls, a low double bed with real blankets and the bed-linen was just that. Linen. It was spare, stylish and, in comparison with my single-bedded room at home with its floral wallpaper, shelves full of favourite childhood books and menagerie of stuffed animals—very grown up.

'It's lovely,' I said. Still unwilling to put down my suitcase and spoil the perfection.

'It looks too much like a department store-room setting for my taste. It needs living in.' She glanced at me, standing practically to attention, afraid to touch anything, and grinned. 'Relax, Philly. Don't be afraid to muss it up and make yourself at home.' She crossed the room and threw open another door. 'You've got an *en suite* shower. And this,' she said, ignoring the reality of my ruined suitcase, 'is a walk-in wardrobe.'

It didn't take a theoretical physicist to work out that I didn't need a walk-in anything. A small cupboard would accommodate my limited wardrobe with space left over. But what with a uniform for work and over-alls for the garage—neither of which was needed in London—I was rather short of clothes. My priority had been saving up for a deposit on a home of my own so that when Don eventually realised that there was more to life than old cars there'd be nothing to stop us. I was going to assuage my misery by blowing some of it on some serious working clothes. If I wasn't going to have a personal life for the next six months, I might as well do my career some good.

'Do you want to give me your jacket? I'll hang it up to dry.'

It occurred to me that people who lived in this kind of apartment block couldn't hang out their washing on a line in the back garden. 'Is there a launderette nearby? Some of my…um…clothes got a bit muddy.'

'Possibly, but why go out in the rain when we've got everything you need right here? Washer, dryer and the finest steam iron a divorce settlement can buy.'

A dryer? I quashed the thought that my mother wouldn't approve and grinned. 'Thanks, Kate.'

'You're welcome,' she said. 'Now I'd better go and make sure that my sulky little sister isn't lacing your

tea with something unpleasant. Don't stand on cere-
mony. A bathrobe is as formal as it gets around here
at this time on a Friday.' And she grinned. 'Just fol-
low the sound of Sophie's teeth gnashing when you're
ready.'

CHAPTER THREE

It's dark and raining. Your room-mates have gone out and you're on your own in a strange flat. As you turn on the cooker to prepare some absolutely vital comfort food you blow the fuses. Do you:

a. remember that there's a pub on the corner? You can get something to eat there and find a bloke who knows how to fix a fuse. Excellent.

b. go next door for help? The guy who lives there never leaves the house in daylight, but, hey, it's dark, so that's not a problem.

c. ring the emergency services and cry?

d. keep a torch and spare fuse wire by the fusebox? You fix the fuse yourself.

e. just cry?

'FEELING better?'

Kate was on her own in the kitchen and waved in the direction of the teapot, indicating that I should help myself.

'Much,' I said, although I felt a little self-conscious in my aged bathrobe, with my hair wrapped in one of the thick soft towels that had been left for me. I'd never shared a flat with girls my own age before but

34

I had friends who were quick to tell me that it was a minefield.

Rows over who'd taken the last of the milk, or bread. Rows over telephone bills. And worst of all, rows over men. At least that wouldn't be a problem. I had enough trouble holding my own man's attention against the incomparable glamour of a carburettor, let alone attracting any attention from any of theirs.

Kate seemed friendly enough but I didn't want her to think I was freeloading. 'I need to go shopping, stock up on the essentials, if you'll point me in the direction of the nearest supermarket,' I said as I filled a cup.

'Don't worry tonight. So long as you don't eat Sophie's cottage cheese you'll be fine.'

'No problem,' I said, with feeling, and we both grinned.

'Do you know anyone in London, Philly?'

I shook my head. Then said, 'Well…' Kate waited. 'I met the man who lives next door. We hailed the same taxi and since we were going in the same direction it seemed logical to share. Not that I knew he lived next door then, of course.'

Kate looked surprised. Actually it did seem pretty unlikely, but it wasn't the coincidence that bothered her. 'You got into a taxi with a man you didn't know?'

I was still feeling a little bit wobbly about that myself.

'It was raining. And he was prepared to let me take it. He was really, very…um…' On the point of saying kind, I was assailed by a vivid recollection of impatience barely held in check behind fathoms-deep sea-green eyes. Of his heel grinding my attack alarm in the pavement. Of his sharp 'wait here'. And my mouth dried on 'kind'.

'Yes?'

'Actually, I owe him an apology.' I swallowed. 'And probably a new umbrella.' Kate's brows quirked upwards. 'It's a long story.'

'Then it's one that'll have to keep. I've got a date with a totally gorgeous barrister. I'd have cancelled when I realised you would be arriving today, but I have long-term plans for this one and I'm not risking him out alone on Friday night.' And she grinned as she pushed herself off her stool. 'Don't worry. I'm not leaving you on your own with Sophie. She's going to a party. I would have asked her to take you but, in her present mood, I couldn't positively guarantee you'd have a good time.'

'No,' I said. Relieved. The thought of going to a party, being forced into the company of a roomful of strangers, with or without Sophie, was not appealing.

And when, an hour or so later, Sophie drifted into the kitchen on high, high heels, ethereal in silvery chiffon, a fairy dusting of glitter across her shoulders, her white-blonde hair a mass of tiny waves, the relief intensified.

If I'd walked into a room alongside her fragile beauty, I'd have looked not just like a mouse, but a well-fed country mouse.

'Will you be all right on your own?' Kate asked,

following her, equally stunning in the kind of simple black dress that didn't come from any store that had a branch in Maybridge High Street. 'There's a pile of videos if there's nothing on television you fancy and a list of fast-food outlets that deliver by the phone.' And she grinned. 'We don't cook if we can help it.'

'I'll be fine,' I said, trying not to dwell on the fact that, for the first time in as long as I could remember on a Friday night, Don would not be bounding up to my front door ready to fall in with whatever I'd planned for the evening. Even if it did involve sitting through a chick-flick. I tried not to picture him down the pub with his car-crazy mates—no doubt encouraged by his miraculously restored mother not to 'sit at home and brood'. Instead I gestured ironically in the direction of the washing machine where my knickers were going through the rinse cycle. 'I've got plenty to do.'

Kate laughed. 'Whatever turns you on,' she said as the bell rang from the front entrance.

'Come on, Kate, that'll be the taxi,' Sophie said, with a pitying glance in my direction before she went to let the driver know they were on their way.

But Kate hesitated, turned back, the slightest frown creasing her lovely forehead. 'Was it Gorgeous George or Wee Willy?'

'Sorry?'

'Did you share a taxi with George or Willy?'

On the point of explaining that we hadn't actually exchanged names, I realised how lame that sounded. On the other hand, while neither name seemed to suit my unfortunate Galahad, no one in their right mind would have referred to him as Wee Willy...

'Gorgeous George?' I repeated. A question, rather than an answer.

'Tall, dark—'

'That's the one,' I said.

'And very, very gay.'

'Gay?'

She gave me an old-fashioned look that suggested I might be even more of a hick than I looked. 'You didn't realise?'

Gay? He was gay?

No, I hadn't realised. I'd been too busy falling into his hypnotic green eyes...

I pulled myself together, managed a shrug. 'I wasn't paying that much attention,' I said. 'And he was more interested in chasing his umbrella. In fact I should make sure he found it. Which side does he live on?'

Not that I intended to do more than put my apology—along with an offer to pay for repairs or a replacement—in writing and slip it beneath his door. He would undoubtedly take the hint and respond in kind. After that, if we ever passed in the hall, neither of us would have to do more than nod, which would be a relief all round, I told myself.

'Out of the door, turn right. End of the hall. Number seventy-two.' Then she grinned and said, 'Don't wait up.'

'*Gorgeous* George?' I repeated as the door banged shut behind Kate and Sophie. Trying to get my head round the idea. Trying to work out quite why my heart was sinking like a stone.

Clearly it had nothing to do with the man who lived next door. It had to be because I was alone on a Friday night in a city where I had no friends. My parents were thirty thousand feet above terra firma in another time zone and the man in my life, if he wasn't cosied up with his beloved car, was down the pub having a good time without me.

So I did what I always did when I felt down. I opened the fridge.

What I needed—and urgently—was food. But Sophie could relax; her cottage cheese was safe from me. I wanted comfort food.

A bacon and egg sandwich. Or sausages. Something warm, and satisfying and packed with heart-clogging cholesterol. If it was clogged, it wouldn't feel so empty.

But no such luck. The fridge was a fat-free zone.

Then I opened the dairy drawer and hit the jackpot. Either Sophie had a secret vice, or Kate was a girl after my own heart.

There was a pack of expensive, unsalted butter—the kind that tasted like cream spread on bread—and a great big wedge of farmhouse Cheddar cheese from a shop near Covent Garden that I'd read about in the food section of the Sunday paper. I broke a piece off to taste. And drooled.

I passed on the butter. I didn't need butter. Cheese on toast would do very nicely.

It wouldn't be a hardship to take a trip to Covent

Garden in the morning and replace it. I could buy my own supply at the same time and take a look around. Cheered at the idea, I turned on the grill and put the bread to toast on one side. Then I hunted through the cupboards until I found some chilli powder.

Excellent.

It was past its sell-by date—well, Kate had said they didn't cook. From the state of the cupboards, she did not exaggerate. But I wasn't going to get food poisoning from geriatric spice. I'd just have to use more.

I turned back to the stove to check the toast, but the grill hadn't come on and, realising that the cooker was turned off at the main switch, I reached across the worktop and flipped it down.

Several things happened at once.

There was a blue flash, a loud bang and everything went dark. Then I screamed.

It was nothing really over the top as screams went.

It was loud, but nowhere near the ear-rending decibels expected of the heroine in a low-budget horror movie. I was startled—knee-tremblingly, heart-poundingly startled. Not scared witless.

It was also pointless since there was no one around to respond with sympathy for my plight.

I was on my own. Totally on my own. For the first time in my life, there wasn't a soul I could call on for help. I stood there in total darkness, gripping the work surface as if my life depended on it, while my heart gradually slowed to its normal pace and I made a very determined effort not to feel sorry for myself.

I'd blown a fuse. It wasn't the end of the world.

It just felt like it.

Beyond the windows, on the far side of the river, the lights of London twinkled back at me, mockingly. They knew I was out of my depth.

Back home all I'd have to do was pick up the phone and call Don. Not that I'd need him to mend the fuse, but his presence would have been a comfort. And how often did I have the perfect excuse to have him alone with me in a totally empty house? A dark empty house.

His mother might suspect me of planning to take unfair advantage of her precious son, but she wouldn't be able to do a thing about it. Not in an emergency. Not without showing her true colours. And she was too clever for that.

But I wasn't in Maybridge and Don didn't live next door.

Next door lived a man who'd seen my underwear. Which was more than Don had managed in the best part of thirteen years.

That it was plain, serviceable, *ordinary* underwear should have made it marginally less embarrassing, but somehow the fact that he knew I wore boring knickers only made things worse.

Why, I had no idea. He was gay. He wasn't in the slightest bit interested in my underwear, except perhaps aesthetically.

Why was I even thinking about him?

I didn't *need* anybody. I could mend a fuse. All I had to do was find the fuse box.

The cloak cupboard by the door was the most likely place and, keeping hold of the work surfaces, I edged around the kitchen until I found the door. Then, feeling my way along the wall, I set off in what I hoped was the direction of the front door.

It would have been easier if there had been some light. At home we kept candles and matches under the kitchen sink for 'emergencies'. I might have teased my mother about her obsession with 'emergencies', but, while I wasn't about to admit that I really, really wanted her right now, in the thick blackness of the windowless hall I'd have warmly welcomed a little of her forward planning.

What I got was a shin-height table and the expensive sound of breaking porcelain as I flailed wildly to save myself from falling.

It had to be expensive. Everything about this flat was expensive, from its location to its smallest fitting. I was lucky to be living here, even temporarily, I knew—my mother had told me so. At that precise moment I didn't feel lucky. I felt like screaming again.

I didn't. Instead I rubbed my painful shins and considered my options.

I could pack and leave before Sophie and Kate got home.

I could hide the broken crocks—along with the evidence of my attempts at cooking—in my suitcase, go to bed and act surprised in the morning when nothing worked.

I could cry.

Actually, I was closer to tears than at any time since my grandmother had died. But all tears did was make your eyes and nose red, so I resisted the urge to sit on the horrible table and bawl my eyes out. Instead, I edged my way carefully past the broken china and made it to the cloak cupboard without further mishap.

I'd thought it was dark in the hall. In the cupboard it was black.

At home—and at this point I was beginning to realise that I'd seriously underrated my mother—there would have been a torch handily placed on top of the fuse-box, along with spare fuse wire.

'Mum,' I said, lifting my face in the darkness so that she could hear me better. 'I swear I'll never call you a fussy old bat ever again.' Not that I ever had—well, not to her face. 'I'll wear warm underwear without being nagged, replace my attack alarm first thing tomorrow and never, ever go out without a clean handkerchief…just, please, please, let there be a torch with the fuse box.' I groped in the darkness.

There was no torch.

I was released from the warm underwear promise—not that it mattered because the way my life was going no one was ever going to see it *in situ*—but I was still in the dark. Fortunately, the cloak cupboard was right by the front door and it occurred to me that, since I was now living in a luxury apartment, I could borrow some light from the well-lit communal hallway.

Pleased with myself, I opened the door and

screamed again—this time with no holds barred—as a tall figure, silhouetted in black against the light, reached out for me.

Sound-blasted back by my scream, he retreated into the light and I belatedly recognised the neighbour I least wanted to meet. And he hadn't been reaching out to grab my throat as my lurid imagination had suggested, but to ring the doorbell.

It was the first time I'd seen him in full light and there was nothing about him to suggest that my earlier assessment of him had been wrong. He was tall, he was dark. And the way my heart was pumping confirmed that he was, without doubt, dangerous. To my equilibrium, if nothing else.

But what really held my attention was the large flat carton balanced on the palm of his hand. He might be dangerous but he'd got pizza and my stomach—anticipating the promised cheese on toast—responded with an excited gurgle.

'Yes?' I demanded, to cover my embarrassment.

'You screamed,' he said.

'You scared me,' I snapped back as, for the second time in as many minutes, I waited for my heart to steady. Then, 'What do you want?'

'Not just now when you opened the door,' he said, with the careful speech of a man who believed he was dealing with an idiot. 'You screamed a minute or two ago—'

A minute or two? It seemed as if I'd been in the dark for hours...

'—and since I saw your friends go out, I thought

I'd better make sure you're not just watching a scary video alone in the dark.'

'Oh,' I said. It was just as well I wasn't trying to impress this man. He clearly thought I was a total ditz. 'Sorry. I didn't realise the walls were so thin.'

'They're not.' He said this with the authority of a man who knew. 'I was at my door when you—'

He seemed reluctant to use the word again and I could scarcely blame him. 'Screamed,' I said, rescuing him. 'I'm sorry to have disturbed you. The fuses blew. That's all.' *All!* 'I was just going to fix them.'

'You know how?' he said, without bothering to disguise his disbelief.

I tried to remember that he was being kind. A good neighbour. That he could have just shut his door. 'They teach girls stuff like that in school these days,' I assured him.

'Really?' He seemed unimpressed but he didn't argue. Didn't do that 'I'm a big clever man and you're just a girl' thing that most men did. Instead he said, 'Well, I'll leave you to it.' Which should have been more gratifying than it was. He took a step in the direction of his own front door, then hesitated, turned back. 'You've got spare fuse wire?'

There had been none where I'd have expected it to be and it occurred to me that I might yet be grateful for his 'good neighbour' act.

'I shouldn't think so for a minute,' I said. Keeping my smile to myself.

'No,' he said. 'I've only seen your flatmates from

a distance. Very decorative, but they didn't strike me as the practical type.'

I considered the fragile beauty of Sophie, the cool sophistication of Kate. 'You may be right,' I said. Women who looked like that would never need to be practical.

'Why don't you see if you can find the blown fuse while I fetch some wire?' he suggested.

'Actually, a screwdriver would be useful,' I said. 'If you've got one.'

'A screwdriver. Right.'

'And perhaps a torch?'

He said nothing, just handed me the pizza and left me to it, which, considering the way my stomach had rumbled, was trusting of him. But I resisted the urge to open the box, grab a slice and eat it before he returned. Instead I used the time to recover my wits— and my breath—as well as find the fuse. Although why he should leave me so completely breathless was a mystery.

He was gay, I reminded myself.

And I was practically engaged to quite tall, fair-haired and safe Don. We were Philly-and-Don. Had been for as long as I could remember. Everyone considered us a couple. Except his mother, of course. How she must be enjoying my banishment.

I put the pizza down on the hall table and by the time my new neighbour returned, with wire, a small screwdriver and a torch, I'd located the fuse. 'What blew it?' he asked, handing me the wire, his fingers brushing mine in the process. Which undid all the good work I'd put in on my breathing while he'd been fetching it and I dropped the fuse. 'Do you know?'

'The cooker,' I said, bending down quickly to retrieve it. Which could have explained why my cheeks were hot.

'I'd better make sure it's turned off.'

His passage to the kitchen was punctuated by a crunching sound as his huge feet crushed delicate pottery into the polished floor. He muttered something under his breath that I didn't quite catch. I didn't ask him to repeat it. I had a feeling that what he'd said was not for my benefit, but simply to relieve his own feelings.

'Okay,' he said, when he returned. 'The cooker is off. You'd better get someone to check it out before you try to use it again.'

I hadn't actually been planning a rerun of the last ten minutes, but all I said was, 'There goes my cheese on toast.' Then, busy with the fuse wire, 'Why did you bring the pizza with you?'

I couldn't believe I'd said that. I might as well have sat up and begged, my tongue hanging out, drooling.

'I was paying the delivery man at the door when I heard your—exclamation of annoyance. I thought your safety was more important than eating my supper while it was still hot. I'd have been quicker but the delivery man refused to wait for his money.'

I glanced up, certain he was being sarcastic.

He used the opportunity to take the fuse from me and check it out before handing it back. It was an action that would, under normal circumstances, have infuriated me, but I suspected the fit of trembling that swept through me had more to do with the way his fingers brushed against mine in the semi-darkness than outraged feminism.

Not that I wasn't furious; I was.

Before I could gather myself for a serious tantrum, however, he said, 'Maybe you'd care to share it with me?'

Share? Share what?

'I realise pizza is no substitute for cheese on toast, but it's as near as you're going to get tonight without a cooker.'

It was odd. He wasn't smiling and yet it felt as if he were.

I turned quickly away, my fingers fumbling with the fuse as I turned to push it into its slot.

It wasn't just the long fingers, it was the gravelly voice, I decided. It was terminally sexy.

The hallway was flooded with light and for a moment I was left blinking like a mole emerged from the dark. When my eyes had recovered from the shock, I realised he was holding out his hand.

'I'm Callum McBride,' he said, rather formally. Then, 'Cal.'

He had long, thin fingers, strong and scarred with hard use. They were the kind of fingers that looked as if they could do anything. Lay bricks, play a sonata, gentle a baby to sleep.

I just didn't get it.

Despite all recent evidence to the contrary, I wasn't totally stupid. I had friends in Maybridge who were gay. They didn't wear placards around their necks, but I hadn't needed the facts to be spelled out in words of one syllable despite the fact that some of them had looks that would turn any girl's head. They just didn't get this kind of purely female response from me. The kind you got when a man and a woman looked at one another and wanted to rip their clothes off.

So what was there about him that Kate and Sophie could see, but that I was missing?

Then the name registered.

'Callum? Callum McBride. You're not Gorgeous George?' I said, with a rush of relief. It was all a mistake. A huge mistake…

'Gorgeous George?' he repeated.

'Kate described you as tall, dark and g-g-gorgeous,' I said, stopping myself from using the 'gay' word just in time. I'd made enough of a fool of myself for one day. And he'd probably be terminally offended, ignore me in the lift for the rest of my stay. 'I wanted to put a note through your letterbox but I didn't know your name. From her description I assumed you must be George from number seventy-two…'

Something in his eyes warned me that my mouth was wide open and my foot was jammed right in it. It was at that point I realised that 'Gorgeous George' was just Kate and Sophie's nickname for him. Like 'Wee Willy'.

And now he knew it too.

'Oh, knickers,' I said. 'You do live at number seventy-two, don't you?'

'That's me. Tall, dark and g-g-gorgeous?' His almost-smile suggested he knew that gorgeous hadn't been my first choice of word. 'And you are?'

I was an idiot. Why else would his fingers against my skin be sending tiny shock waves of pleasure to my brain?

'I'm Philly Gresham,' I said, 'and now I'm going to the kitchen to kill myself.'

I made a move to take my hand from his, but his grip tightened imperceptibly, holding me fast. 'Don't do that. Not until you've helped me eat this pizza.'

He wasn't offended? Apparently not. The almost-smile finally reached his eyes and as they crinkled at the corners my abdomen tightened in response. I recognised the feeling. Anticipation, excitement, a promised treat.

I like pizza, but it doesn't usually have that effect on me.

'Purely as a penance?' I asked.

'Oh, well, if it's penance you want, you'll have to share a bottle of wine with me, too.'

'Boy,' I said, 'you're tough.'

'But g-g-gorgeous with it,' he said. And then he grinned. 'Why don't you pick up the broken china while I go and fetch a bottle from next door?'

I tore my gaze from his face and glanced at the mess. 'Do you think it'll stick back together?'

'I shouldn't think so for a minute,' he said, repeating my own words back at me, his eyes alight with amusement before he turned to retrace his steps to his own apartment. The one with number seventy-two on the door.

So, he really was gay.

Until I saw him open his front door, I hadn't realised how much I wanted to be wrong about that.

The little heart-sink moment of regret was pure selfishness, I knew. Sheer arrogance to think that he was the one missing out. I don't suppose he thought that for one moment.

Cal McBride had been, was being, kind and suddenly London looked a lot more welcoming.

Okay, as I picked up the broken china I admit that I did have a momentary qualm about Don. But only a momentary one. After all, he had his Austin to keep him company. And Cal, well, Cal wasn't interested in me as a woman. Which was actually rather splendid. Perfect, in fact. We could be true friends without any of that tiresome boy/girl stuff. No guilt.

Besides, I was hungry.

For one reckless moment I considered suggesting that we ate our supper in front of the television, to the accompaniment of that scary video. Something stopped me. Perhaps it was the sure and certain knowledge that the only reason I'd ever watch a scary video was for the opportunity it gave me to throw myself into the arms of the man in my life.

I'd been doing a lot of that lately.

Once Don had spent two or three hours in the garage working on the car, a bowl of microwave popcorn and late-night video on the sofa was about as energetic as he got.

That had to be why he'd been so slow to take advantage of the opportunities I'd kept throwing in his way. All he did was put one comforting arm around me, leaving the other free to dig into the popcorn.

To be honest, I was beginning to wonder if his witch of a mother was putting something in his food to suppress his natural urges. She grew her own herbs, drying them in great bunches in her kitchen, and who knew what they were and what she did with them?

But at least I could describe Don as 'the man in my life' and get no argument.

Callum McBride wasn't ever going to be that. So there was no point in scaring myself to death for nothing.

Absolutely not.

CHAPTER FOUR

You break a valuable ornament while staying in the home of people you've only just met. Do you:
a. immediately own up, apologise and forget it, assuming it's properly insured?
b. panic and attempt to repair it with instant glue?
c. leave the pieces for someone else to find?
d. blame any pet larger than a stick insect?
e. move heaven and earth in an effort to replace it before they notice?
f. call a cab from your mobile phone, pack your bag and leave by the back door?

'ANCHOVIES!'

I'd busied myself finding napkins and glasses, showing uncharacteristic restraint in the matter of the pizza. I hadn't even peeked to see what toppings Cal had picked. I wasn't really fussy and at that moment anything would have been welcome, but I had to admit to a real weakness for anchovies.

I'd left the door on the latch and after a few minutes he returned with a bottle of red wine, so dark that it was almost purple. I regarded it with misgiving as he filled the glasses. I didn't drink much. A spritzer when Don and I went down the pub, that was all. The only time I'd ever had a glass of red wine, I'd had a terrible headache the following day so I'd never repeated the experience. I didn't say anything, though. It would be rude. I'd just take a sip.

He nodded in the direction of the box. 'Dig in.'

I didn't need telling twice, but flipped open the box and instantly forgot my concern about the wine as I spotted my favourite food. Cal had gone for classic simplicity. With anchovies. And extra olives.

'You can pick them off if you don't like them,' Cal said and I realised that my exclamation could have been taken as easily for horror as delight.

'You've got to be kidding,' I said, helping myself and catching the oozing strings of mozzarella on my fingers, taking it straight to my mouth. Okay, so it wasn't pretty, but there was no other way to eat that kind of stuff. 'My boyfriend hates anchovies,' I said, after a long sigh of contentment. 'This is a real treat.'

He hooked his foot around a stool, pulled it back and sat next to me. As he reached for a slice of pizza his arm brushed against my shoulder and I jumped as if I'd had an electric shock. He glanced back at me, curbing his own rush to sink his teeth into the deep and crispy crust.

'Boyfriend?'

'Don,' I said. 'Don Cooper. He lives next door.'

'No, he doesn't,' he said, before finally taking a bite out of his delayed supper. I frowned. 'I live next door.'

'Oh, well, yes,' I said. And laughed, but more as a

defence mechanism than from any real amusement. He was about as much like a 'boy next door' as I was like Kate and Sophie. 'Obviously I meant he lives next door to me at home. In Maybridge.'

'That's—'

'A cliché. I know.' I said it before he did. I'd been teased by my older brothers and sister for years. I'd been teased by my friends. I was beyond embarrassing on the subject. Or at least I thought I was. 'Falling for the boy next door is the world's biggest cliché, but he moved in when I was ten and he was twelve and it's been Philly-and-Don ever since. Side by side. No spaces.' I shrugged. 'Except for his mother. As far as she's concerned we're Philippa and Donald. Preferably with a five metre wide ditch between the little "a" and the capital "D".'

'She doesn't like you?' His eyes narrowed thoughtfully. As if he understood where she was coming from.

'I don't think it's that personal. I don't think she'd like any girl who had plans to take her son away from her.'

'She'll be glad you've moved to London, then.' The corner of Cal's mouth lifted imperceptibly. I'd have said it was a wry smile, except it stopped just short of the smile.

'Turning cartwheels, I shouldn't wonder.' But only when no one could see.

'What about Don? He must be pretty fed up that you're hitting the bright lights without him.'

Not nearly fed up enough. Just envious of the fact

that I'd get to see the original of his car in the Science Museum. That was my business, though.

'He's reached a critical point in the restoration of a 1922 Austin Seven,' I explained. 'I'm a distraction.'

'That I can believe,' he said. With feeling.

'Look—I'm really sorry about earlier. Your umbrella, the alarm… I'll pay for any repairs. Was it badly damaged?' He looked confused. I didn't blame him. So little time, so many disasters. 'Your umbrella.'

'If I ever find it I'll let you know.'

'Oh…sugar.' I glanced at the pile of thin porcelain I'd put into a dish, hoping, against the odds, that I might be able to do something with it. Or, failing that, to find a matching replacement. But while the original break might have been reparable, nothing that fragile was ever going to survive a close encounter with Cal's feet—however elegantly shod. 'I'm not having a very good day.'

'No.' Then, 'Why didn't you wait for me?'

I'd been hoping he wouldn't bring that up. 'Simple kindness?' I offered. 'I'd stolen your taxi, lost your umbrella and gone a fair way to shattering your eardrums. I thought you deserved a break.'

He was supposed to smile. He didn't. 'You managed your suitcase all right on your own?'

That was why he'd told me to wait? So that he could help? After all that… 'No problem,' I said. Wishing I'd stayed after all. Then, 'Why didn't you tell me that you lived in the same block? When I told you where I was going? I thought…'

Actually, I didn't want to tell him what I'd thought, but he was way ahead of me.

'I thought you wouldn't believe me. That you might think I was coming on to you.'

'Oh...' I said. 'No-o-o...'

His smile suggested that I was fooling no one but what he said was, 'You took quite a risk, you know.' His gaze held mine for a moment. 'Something that you clearly realised, if somewhat belatedly. That *was* why you were holding an attack alarm in your pocket?'

'Mmm,' I said, noncommittally. It occurred to me that I still was. Taking a risk. It would certainly account for a raised pulse rate and curiously erratic heartbeat. Then, to cover my own confusion, I picked up the piece of broken china that bore the potter's mark. 'Do you think I'll be able to replace this without going bankrupt?'

He continued to look at me for what seemed like for ever, before finally taking the piece of shattered porcelain, glancing at the imprint. His expression did not fill me with optimism.

'Don't worry. It'll be insured,' he said.

That was supposed to reassure me?

'Oh, great. I've been foisted on the Harrington girls as a charity case and on the day I arrive I blow the fuses and smash a valuable bowl.'

'The fuse wasn't your fault, just bad luck. And you fixed it.'

'With your help.'

'That's what neighbours are for. And as long as it's

fixed they won't worry about the details.' He picked up a glass and offered it to me. 'Stop fretting and take a swig of that. It'll make you feel that the world is a better place.'

I looked at it doubtfully. 'I don't usually drink red wine.'

'You should do one new thing every day.' He placed the glass in my hand, wrapping his long fingers around mine to steady it. Honestly, though, he was just making things worse.

I didn't normally shake like this. It had to be this extraordinary closeness that seemed more than physical, this intimacy with a stranger that not even the clinical décor of the kitchen, the bright lighting and the sheer banality of the conversation could diminish.

He just seemed to affect me that way. Make me edgy, jumpy and a little bit excited as our eyes locked over the glass.

'I think I might have overdrawn on the ''new thing'' bank today,' I said, my voice slightly hoarse.

'Trust me, Philly. You can't overdraw.'

'No?' Maybe not. 'Well, maybe you're right. And I do have a lot of catching up to do.'

With Don I was comfortable, easy. Best friends. As my big sister was fond of remarking, we were like a couple who'd been married for thirty years. Of course, she hadn't meant it as a compliment.

Right now, with Cal holding my hands between his, I felt as if I was standing on the edge of a precipice and that was very new, so I quickly ducked my head to drink the wine. It slid down my throat, spreading through me, warming me. And he was right. I did feel better.

'Gosh, that's good,' I said and took a second mouthful.

'Liquid sunshine,' he agreed, and finally let go. The heat evaporated and I was left with the disconcerting impression that the warmth had come direct from him, not the wine. I sipped again, but the effect was diminished and I put the glass down and returned to the safer comfort of pizza.

'You don't know the Harrington girls?' Cal said, after a moment or two. 'I assumed you must be old school friends or something.'

'Did you?' He'd been thinking about me? 'Er, no,' I said. Any thoughts he'd had about me wouldn't be flattering. 'My mother is on a committee with their mother's cousin,' I explained. 'Or maybe my mother's cousin is on a committee with their mother...' I found myself frowning and, since it wasn't in the least bit important, I let it go. 'You've heard of the old boys' network? Well, this is the old girls' version. I needed somewhere to stay. They had a spare room. Bingo,' I said. And giggled. Which was odd, since he'd just reminded me that I'd have to spend the next six months being scowled at by Sophie and I didn't feel much like laughing.

'Right.'

'Not really,' I said, lowering my voice. 'Sophie wanted the room for a man she's got designs on.' I reached for a second slice of pizza and then, remembering my manners, glanced at Cal.

'Help yourself,' he said, and refilled my glass.

I didn't need telling twice. 'Do you think she might have booby-trapped the cooker to get rid of me? Sophie…' I added, when he raised his eyebrows. Good grief, what was I saying? Rapidly changing the subject, I said, 'This is so-o-o good. Don always orders the meat feast. You know…piled high with, um, meat. Pepperoni and stuff. The kind with a single olive in the middle if you're lucky.' I took one of the olives and popped it in my mouth. 'And no anchovies. Which is okay,' I said, quickly, realising that I was repeating myself. 'But this makes a lovely change,' I finished lamely, and then decided my mouth would be more usefully employed in eating.

And for a moment there was silence while we concentrated on the food.

'What do you do when you're in Maybridge? Apart from distract Don,' Cal asked, after a while.

'My job?' That was safer territory. The kind of polite, social, conversational gambit I was comfortable with. And I gratefully followed his lead, telling him about the bank and the people who worked there. The sweet customers who brought me cakes. The cheeky ones who flirted and asked me out. The weird ones whom I wasn't sorry to leave behind.

'Are you looking for the same kind of thing in London? Or have you got a transfer to a different branch?'

'A transfer of sorts. Just a temporary one.' I glanced sideways at him. 'What do you do when you're not rescuing drowning damsels? And chasing umbrellas.'

'I make films. Documentaries,' he added quickly, before I could get too excited and throw myself on the nearest couch. 'Wildlife stuff.'

'In London?' I asked, without thinking. Then, realising my mistake, 'Oh, no…'

'Oh, yes. I've made films in London. Urban foxes. Feral cats.' He grinned. 'The secret life of the pigeon.'

'Really?' I tried to sound thrilled. I'd been imagining polar bears, lions, wolves. Oh, well. 'I didn't realise the pigeon had a secret life. I thought it did absolutely everything in the street,' I said. Then wished I hadn't.

'Of course, I do have to do boring stuff, too. I've just come back from the Serengeti. We've been making a film about a year in the life of a family of cheetahs—'

'That's boring?' He grinned. 'Oh, you're teasing.'

My brothers had teased me, when they'd been at home. Don used to, but lately he'd been distracted by the Austin and I'd apparently lost the ability to spot one coming.

'You like to travel?' I asked.

'I can't pretend it's all wonderful, but, yes, I enjoy seeing new places. Don't you?'

'My brothers and sister are the travellers in our family. They got to the family gene bank first and emptied the "travel and adventure" account.' Then I shrugged. 'And I don't fly.'

'Me neither. I usually take a plane...' His voice trailed off as I just stared at him. 'Sorry. Not funny. So you're going to stay at home and marry Don?'

The way he said it made me sound about as interesting as watching paint dry. 'That's the plan,' I said, firmly.

Well, it was my plan. In my head I had it planned down to the last hand-stitched pearl on my cream silk train. I was a redhead, okay? I looked better in cream than white. And I wouldn't want anyone to think I was a virgin. It was bad enough being one.

Don hadn't actually got around to getting down on one knee and asking me, but everyone assumed that we'd get married. Not that I had a diamond on my left hand. And no one was getting flustered about invitations, or bridesmaids. With my parents away for six months nothing was going to happen on that front any time soon.

'Eventually,' I added before he asked when the wedding was going to take place.

'Is he in engineering?' Dragged from my this-year, next-year, sometime, never thoughts, I frowned.

'Engineering?'

'I thought perhaps he might be an engineer. With his interest in cars.'

'Oh. Oh, no. He's an accountant. It's the family business. His grandfather was an accountant. His father was an accountant until he ran away with his secretary to run a smallholding in Wales. His uncles and cousins are—'

'Accountants,' Cal said.

'Right. He'll be a partner eventually. The car is just a hobby.'

'Is it?' We both reached for the same piece of pizza. Our hands collided and mine retreated like a snail's antennae. He pushed the box towards me as if he hadn't noticed. 'That's some hobby,' he said.

'Oh, Don's always enjoyed fixing things up. He started by rebuilding a wrecked bike he found in a skip just after he moved in next door. He brought it home, but then realised he didn't have any tools—'

'His father would have needed them in Wales,' Cal said.

He was quick. And he was paying attention. He'd just better not be smiling. I gave a quick glance in his direction. He wasn't...

'I used to smuggle my Dad's toolbox to him through a hole in the fence.'

'That was handy.' This time there was a tell-tale lift to the corner of his mouth.

'It wasn't very subtle, was it?' But a girl had to do what a girl had to do. 'My reward was to be allowed to help him polish the spokes.'

'The way to a man's heart has many paths.'

'This one became so well worn that my Dad eventually put a gate there.' I wondered, briefly, what the new tenants would make of that. Then I shrugged. 'Since then,' I said, 'the projects have just got bigger. More complex.'

And lately, a lot more time-consuming.

For a while Cal said nothing. Just stared into his glass. 'I found an old Super-8 movie camera in the attic when I was a kid. I thought it was magic.' And he smiled at the child he'd been. 'I took a sheet from the airing cupboard to build a hide in the garden for filming birds. It was white so I painted it with some creosote I found in the shed. I nearly killed myself with the fumes. And then my mother nearly killed me for ruining one of her best linen sheets.'

'She must be proud of you now.'

'Must she? My grandfather was an architect. She's an architect. My uncles and my cousins are all architects. She married an architect.' He drained his glass and slid from the stool. 'I'd better go.'

The sudden movement took me by surprise. 'Must you? I could make coffee.'

'Thanks, but I don't think it would be wise to touch any of the switches until the electrics have been checked over. I'll get someone along first thing tomorrow to look at it.'

'You don't have to do that.'

'It's no trouble.' He turned in the kitchen doorway. 'And if you insist on replacing that broken bowl, I'll take you to Portobello Road. The flea market is on Saturday and you might find something like it there.' About to say that he shouldn't judge me on my performance today, that I was perfectly capable of doing all of those things for myself, I stopped myself. Just because I could do it by myself didn't mean I had to. 'Can you be ready by ten o'clock?' he asked, already halfway through the door.

Ten o'clock? That was halfway through the day. 'No problem. Thank you, Cal. And thank you for…'

But he was gone. I heard the front door close with the well-bred clunk of an expensive lock. And I was alone. But no longer lonely, I discovered. 'Everything,' I finished.

If I'd thought about what kind of night I might have in a strange bed, in a strange flat, in a strange town, I'd have assumed it would have been disturbed, restless. But having washed the glasses, dumped the empty—empty? What happened to my resolution to stick at a sip?—wine bottle in the bin with the pizza carton, I sank into the huge bed, oblivious to my tasteful surroundings, and remembered no more until I was woken by a long peal on the doorbell.

I sat up with a start and then wished I hadn't as something inside my head exploded. And the evening came rushing back to me.

Power cut. Cal McBride. Pizza. Cal McBride. Red wine.

The sickening feeling that accompanied the thought 'red wine' left me in no doubt where the headache had come from. And I sank back against the pillows.

The doorbell was attacked again and this time it was held down. Since there was no other way to stop it, I crawled out of bed and peered out into the hall. No one else had stirred. Desperate for silence, I unlocked the door and opened it a crack.

The noise of the bell abruptly stopped. 'Sorry to disturb you so early, Philly, but I've brought the electrician.'

I blinked, pushed the hair out of my eyes. Cal was

at the door and he was not alone. His companion was wearing blue overalls, had a businesslike toolbox clamped in his hand, and I realised that some response was called for.

'You woke me up,' I said. It was the first thing that came into my head. And I looked at my watch to underline my complaint. It seemed to be telling me that it was just after eight, but I couldn't quite focus on the tiny numbers.

'It's now or Thursday week,' the electrician said. 'Please yourself.' And he took a step back as if to say that, if I didn't want him, there were plenty of others who'd be glad to pay his weekend call-out charge.

'Now!' Cal said, in a voice that suggested no one had better disagree with him.

'Now!' I echoed, rather more feebly, opening the door wider before he could walk away with the cocky assurance that only a skilled artisan in high demand could carry off. Then I clutched at my head. 'Sorry. I'm not thinking straight. I'm not used to red wine.'

The electrician shook his head, in a practised you-young-girls manner. I almost expected him to tut. But he restrained himself and, without waiting for an invitation, walked in, found the fuse-box and threw the switch to isolate the mains before heading for the kitchen.

Cal remained where he was. His name might not be George, but he did look absolutely gorgeous in close-fitting jeans that were moulded to the kind of thighs any footballer would have been proud of. And a dark blue collarless shirt that gave his eyes a more Mediterranean than Atlantic hue.

'Thank you,' I said. 'Despite all evidence to the contrary, I really appreciate this.'

'You're welcome.'

Still he didn't move.

'I'd offer you a cup of coffee—I could really use a cup of coffee—but the electricity is off,' I said, unnecessarily. He already knew that.

'Why don't you come next door and I'll make coffee for both of us?' he offered, cheering me up considerably.

'If you throw in a couple of painkillers, you've got a deal.'

'You've got a headache?' he asked, concerned. And, without waiting for an answer, he reached out to push back the explosive mop of hair that was covering my eyes and laid his hand on my forehead. It was blissfully cool and my headache magically vanished.

'I'm sorry. I don't drink much,' I admitted.

'It isn't something to apologise for,' he said, which made me feel better still. Then he took his hand away, which didn't. But he only moved it as far as my wrist, wrapping his long fingers about it in order to lead me next door, apparently concerned I couldn't see where I was going through my hair.

But I hesitated. 'Hadn't I better tell Sophie and Kate?'

'Why? They're not invited,' he said. 'I'm not responsible for their hangovers. Just yours.'

'I haven't got a hangover,' I said, too quickly and too loudly. I closed my eyes, ran my tongue over dry lips. The headache relief had been temporary. 'I just wish I'd stuck to one glass of wine.'

'Put a pound in a jar,' he advised. 'And do it every time you say that. You'll be a rich woman in no time.'

'No, I won't. The situation isn't going to arise again.' He didn't look convinced but I wasn't giving him an opportunity to say so. 'I just thought that Sophie and Kate might wonder where I am.'

'I very much doubt it, Philly. It's Saturday. Assuming one or either of them came home last night, they won't surface much before midday. But leave them a note if you think they'll send out a search party for you.'

'No…I meant…' Actually I wasn't sure what I did mean. 'I'd better get dressed.'

'Must you?'

Something in his eyes alerted me to the fact that I might be reliving the embarrassment of this moment for the rest of my life and, with the greatest reluctance, I looked down.

I was wearing a washed thin rugby shirt that had once belonged to one of my brothers. When new it had been quartered in colours bright enough to shine through the mud of a rugby scrum and long enough to reach almost to my knees. Years of hard washing had reduced it to pastel shades and it now skimmed my thighs just the right side of decency.

Wearing it was rather like eating an egg and bacon

sandwich. A 'comfort' thing. Only to be indulged in when there was no chance of anyone seeing you.

Not, of course, that Cal would have been in the slightest bit interested in the unfettered acres of thigh I was displaying. But I was still mortified and I gave a startled groan, jerked my hand from his grasp and shut the door.

If it hadn't been aching quite so much, I would have banged my head against it.

There was a moment of silence before the lightest of taps on the other side informed me that Cal was still there.

I didn't believe there was any chance of him disappearing in a puff of smoke, no matter how hard I wished. And he was going out of his way to be a kind, caring neighbour. So I opened it again, just a crack, keeping my body tucked behind it.

'Bastard,' I said. 'Why didn't you say something?' His look of injured innocence didn't fool me for a moment. 'Go and put on that coffee you're torturing me with while I make myself decent.'

'I'll leave the door on the latch. Just come in when you're ready.' He half turned, then looked back. 'We'll get breakfast out.' He didn't wait for my answer, which was probably just as well.

CHAPTER FIVE

Due to an unfortunate series of mishaps, the totally gorgeous man you've just met believes you're a total idiot. You want to show him that, contrary to appearances, you've got a brain and know how to use it. Do you:

a. do nothing? Once he gets to know you better he'll realise his mistake and you can both laugh about it.

b. swap your contact lenses for those big-frame specs you swore you'd die rather than wear again? They made you look like a geek—but an intelligent geek.

c. invite him into your office so that you can sort out his pension plan and investments? That'll show him.

d. ask yourself if you really want to impress a man who thinks you're an idiot based on such a brief acquaintance? Nothing that happened was really your fault.

e. realise that, since he isn't avoiding you, he must actually like stupid women, and dump him?

I STOOD under the shower and let the hot water and shampoo sluice away the wish-I-hadn't-drunk-that feeling. It was a new day. The first day of my new life as a tiger. Yesterday didn't count. Yesterday it had been raining and my life had been out of my control.

I wanted to forget most of yesterday. Apart from sharing a pizza with Cal, it had been a disaster from start to finish.

He had been the one bright spark in the gloom, although today hadn't got off to such a great start, either. He might have thought it was amusing that I'd opened the door wearing nothing but a shrunken rugby shirt. It wasn't my mission in life to make him laugh. Not at me, anyway.

I'd correct his impression that I was a clown if it was the last thing I did and the first line of attack had to be clothes. I wrapped a towel around me and considered my limited wardrobe.

He'd been wearing jeans, making it easy for me. It was, after all, Saturday and we were going to browse at a flea market, so jeans were good. But this time they'd be a pair that hadn't been abandoned by one of my older siblings, but a pair that I'd bought for myself.

True, they didn't have the kind of label you wore on the outside to tell the world just how expensive they were. They were the kind you cut the label out of so no one would see where you'd bought them. But they were boot-cut to ride over my favourite Chelseas and they fitted me like a glove. A rather tight glove, admittedly. Misery loved chocolate and I'd been very miserable for the last couple of weeks.

I breathed in hard. Button and buttonhole finally connected and I slotted a woven leather belt through the loops as a safety precaution, regarding the finished effect with a certain amount of satisfaction. The heavy cream silk shirt I was wearing might have come from the charity shop where my mother helped out two mornings a week, but I wasn't about to tell him that. And my mother was out of the country.

I added a tweed sports jacket that had been around the house for so long I couldn't remember who it had belonged to originally. I'd grabbed it from the coat rack when I'd been in a hurry one day and, since no one had cried foul, I'd kept it. With the addition of a long silk scarf that had belonged to my sister looped around my neck I liked to kid myself that it passed for casual chic. It might have worked if I'd had smooth, sleek hair that flowed down my back.

What I'd got looked more like ginger stuffing that had exploded from a mattress. But a liberal helping of conditioner had tamed the worst excesses of frizz. Of course, it wasn't dry yet. No electricity, no hairdryer.

I glossed my lips, glanced at my back view in the truly scary full-length mirror and sighed. Kidding myself was right.

I checked on the electrician and flinched at the sight of the cooker in pieces. 'I'll, um, be next door if you need me,' I said.

That earned me a look that suggested I was kidding myself again and I beat a hasty retreat.

Cal's door was on the latch. I opened it and heard

the sound of voices. I'd assumed he lived alone, but my assumptions had got me in a lot of trouble lately.

'Er, hello,' I called out.

'We're in the kitchen,' Cal replied.

We? I almost heard my heart hit my boots, but it was too late to change my mind now. If I hadn't thrown a paddy over being seen in my unconventional night attire and allowed him to give me coffee and aspirin when he'd wanted to, I could have made an excuse and ducked out of the expedition to Portobello Road. But I was dressed and ready to go. If I backed out now, he'd know why.

So I put on my bright and happy face—I'd been practising for years on Don's mother so I was really good at this—and headed for the kitchen. Cal turned as I walked in and his brows rose slightly, apparently startled by this total change in demeanour.

'Headache gone?' he asked.

'Washed away under the shower,' I said, brightly, in my best have-a-nice-day manner. He gave me no argument, just handed me a glass of orange juice before making a gesture in the direction of his companion, while continuing to look at me. 'Jay, this is Philly Gresham,' he said, in the briefest of introductions. Adding with a slightly wry smile, 'The girl I was telling you about.'

I got a slight lift of his eyebrows from Jay, which made me wonder what exactly Cal had been saying about me.

'Philly, this is Jay Watson.'

'Hello, Jay.'

'Make it goodbye,' Cal said. 'He's just leaving.'

Jay was indeed wearing an overcoat, but unbuttoned, as if he'd been hoping for an invitation to stay that had never materialised.

'Goodbye, Jay,' I said. Perhaps I should have sounded sorrier to see him go, because he put down the coffee-cup with all the grace of a two-year-old in a sulk, giving me a reproachful look as he headed for the door.

'One o'clock, Cal,' he said. 'Time's short so don't be late.'

I forced down the orange juice and attempted casual sophistication. 'I'm sorry, I seem to have upset your, um...' My brain shrivelled at the thought of what he might be and my mouth dried in sympathy. Cal, pouring coffee into a large bowl-shaped breakfast cup, glanced sideways at me with those unsettling eyes but didn't help me out. 'Partner,' I mumbled.

He retrieved the empty glass and replaced it with the cup of strong black coffee he'd poured. 'Sugar?' he asked, neither confirming nor denying it.

He was looking down at me. His mouth wasn't smiling, but his eyes were creased at the corners as if he found something deeply amusing. I suspected it was me. And my mind went blank. What was it about this man? He could steal my wits, reduce my calm centre to quivering mush with a look.

Taking my silence as 'no', he said, 'Milk?'

I shook my head. And then, just to prove to myself that I remembered how, I said, 'No, thanks. This will be fine.'

To be honest, while I could take or leave milk, I yearned for sugar. I'd been trying to give it up, without any noticeable success, for ages. With my jeans already cutting uncomfortably into my waist, I took this timely loss of my vocal cords as a sign that I'd procrastinated for far too long and I sipped the coffee, making a brave effort not to shudder at the bitterness.

'Look,' I said, making a real effort to get a grip of myself. 'If you're busy I can find my own way to Portobello Road. Despite all appearances to the contrary, I do have two brain cells to rub together.'

'I haven't got a thing to do this morning except replace Jay's precious umbrella.' Which suggested one of two things. He was kind. Or he wasn't convinced by my protestations of mental competence. Maybe he was right to be sceptical. Under the circumstances, only an idiot's heart would be pounding in such an out-of-control way.

Then his words—I'd been overdosing on the gravel-wrapped-in-velvet sound of his voice rather than listening to what he'd said—finally sunk in. 'It was Jay's umbrella?' I said, and I didn't have to pretend to be horrified.

I was quite prepared to dig into my saving-up-to-get-married nest egg to replace Cal's property. He'd been kind. He'd come to my rescue when I was being drenched by the rain. When I'd screamed in the dark.

He'd shared his pizza, for heaven's sake.

I did not feel quite so generous towards Jay. I was still feeling that look he'd given me. It was like a dagger in my back.

The feeling was mutual.

'He insisted on loaning it to me yesterday when I left his place in that downpour despite my protests that I'd probably leave it on the underground. It was, as I've just been told at length, infinitely precious to him and he is not amused by my carelessness.'

I made a determined effort to ignore the stupid niggle of jealousy provoked by that 'when I left his place'—Cal's private life was nothing to do with me—and concentrated on the real issue. 'It wasn't your carelessness. It was mine,' I said. 'No wonder the guy had looked at me as if I was something nasty he'd stepped in.'

Cal didn't give me an argument about that. 'I'm sorry about that. I'd hoped that by telling him the whole story, he might just see the funny side of it.'

'He didn't.'

'No,' he said. 'My mistake.'

I could see how telling your lover you'd loaned his precious umbrella to some woman might not be the greatest move. My only surprise was that he hadn't realised that for himself. 'I'm really sorry.'

Cal smiled. 'Don't be. Just help me choose a peace-offering. There's bound to be a dealer in the Portobello Market and, with luck, we'll find him a suitably precious replacement.'

'Oh, great,' I said. Oh, knickers, I thought. A dealer wouldn't be selling made-in-China knock-offs. He was going to be selling the real thing. Handmade in silk with a gold ferrule and seriously expensive. 'Can we stop by a cash machine on the way?' I asked.

It looked as if I was going to need every penny of my daily limit.

'Notting Hill?' I'd been so impressed by the ease with which Cal negotiated the underground system, causing him considerable amusement as I'd related my own problems the day before, that I hadn't even thought about where we were going. I'd been to London before—shopping, sightseeing, on school trips—but a glimpse of Buckingham Palace from an open-topped bus couldn't compare with the movie-lent glamour of Notting Hill.

'It's the nearest stop,' he said, getting up as the train slid into the station. And I blushed at my open-mouthed excitement to be visiting the real-life film set of one of my favourite films, sincerely glad that Cal had his back to me and was oblivious to my awed excitement.

'Which way?' I asked, looking around me, as we reached street-level.

Cal glanced down at me. 'That depends.'

'What on?'

'Whether you want to buy a book.' And he grinned.

Not oblivious, then. I don't suppose he needed to look at me to know how I was reacting.

'Bother,' I said. 'I was hoping you hadn't noticed my hick-from-the-sticks act.'

'Such a tourist,' he teased.

'Only for the weekend. Next week it gets real.' Then, because I couldn't help myself, 'Is there really a bookstore? Like in the movie?'

'There's a bookstore, but not at all like the one in the movie. It's well run, for one thing. And it specialises in travel books so you wouldn't be interested, would you?'

'A book might inspire me,' I said. And flapped my arms as I grinned right back.

We sat at a corner table in a crowded café in the middle of the antiques market and ordered the kind of traditional, cholesterol-laden breakfast that would strain my waist button to the limit.

The waitress brought us coffee to be going on with. Cal ignored it. He just sat back in his chair, stretching his long legs out in front of him, regarding me as if I were some *objet de vertu* like those I'd seen in the crowded antique shops we'd passed. One he was seriously considering having wrapped up to take home with him.

Just a product of my fevered imagination, of course. Heightened by a slow perusal of bookshelves crammed with travellers' tales with Cal at my back, hand on my shoulder as he'd reached up for a book that had been out of my reach. With Cal buying a book of photographs of the Serengeti and having it gift-wrapped before putting it in my hands with the words, 'Be inspired.'

And then, his arm around my shoulder, keeping me close in the Saturday-morning crowd as we walked through The Lane, cheerful with Christmas lights and the sound of a brass band playing carols, until we reached the café.

Now he was looking at me in a way that Don had never done and, imagination or not, my body was responding eagerly. Yearning to be unwrapped, looked at with pleasure. Touched possessively.

I felt heat spreading through my body in a manner that was shockingly different from the effect caused by my weekly aerobics class. It was a languorous heat. Slow and pleasurable, filling my breasts, stealing through my abdomen…

One new experience every day.

I knew what I'd choose.

'So,' I said abruptly, sitting bolt upright, shocked by the direction my mind had taken. As for the feelings… 'What are you planning to film next?' I asked briskly. 'The fascinating world of the earthworm in a suburban garden? The private life of a rattler in the Arizona desert?' He said nothing, as if he knew exactly what I was doing. 'The nesting habits of the crested newt,' I pressed, a little desperately, determined to get my mind focussed on something that didn't make me want to rip my clothes off.

He took his time about answering, as if his mind were somewhere else. 'Nesting, yes. Newts, no. We're negotiating with one of the networks to film the life cycle of the leatherback turtle,' he said finally, sitting up, letting go of whatever had been holding his thoughts. He spooned sugar into his coffee, stirring it with a lot more concentration than it warranted. 'The cheetah film should help. If Jay ever edits it to his satisfaction.'

'He's a film editor?'

'A brilliant film editor. He takes my films and turns them into art.'

'Well, great.' I should have sounded more enthusiastic, I realised. 'I mean that's good, isn't it?'

'The downside of perfectionism is that he's never satisfied. If I don't stand behind him and push, the final cut won't be delivered on time. So that's my afternoon taken care of. And probably most of the evening.'

If I believed that Jay had an entirely different reason for wanting Cal close at hand, I kept it to myself. It was, I reminded myself, absolutely none of my business. Besides, I was sure he could work that out for himself. He didn't need any help from me.

The little heart-leap of pleasure I felt at his fairly obvious lack of reciprocal enthusiasm was just plain foolishness.

Cal didn't need anything from me.

He was just a friend. He wasn't wafting pheromones in my direction, at least not intentionally, and my reaction to him had nothing to do with sex.

I was simply drawn by his air of sophistication and worldliness. His charm. Those eyes that never seemed to leave my face. The pure novelty of having a man actually giving me his undivided attention.

Heady stuff when I'd spent all my teenage years and my early twenties competing for notice with a long string of broken-down transportation, culminating in Don's drooling obsession with an eighty-year-old car.

'We'd better not waste time,' I said as breakfast—

the old-fashioned kind involving eggs, bacon, sausages and huge black field mushrooms—arrived to distract me. 'You were told not to be late.' And I stared at my plate, wondering how on earth I was going to eat when my appetite had suddenly deserted me.

I jumped as he touched the back of my hand to attract my attention and, startled out of my reverie, I looked up. For a moment he said nothing. Just left his hand on mine, his touch sparking through me like an electric current.

Then he said, 'Will you pass the salt, please?'

Had he asked before and, lost in my own thoughts, I hadn't heard him?

'Too much salt is bad for you,' I said, not moving, not wanting to lose the warmth of his hand against mine.

He looked at the artery-hardening food on his plate and then back to me. 'How much worse can it get?' he asked, his sudden laughter taking me by surprise and breaking the spell. But it was infectious and I found myself grinning back.

'You get the salt,' I said, 'but you have to promise to do something healthy afterwards.'

'Something energetic?'

Energetic suggested images I wasn't prepared to confront. 'A walk would do it,' I said, wishing I'd kept quiet. Then, because that was feeble, 'A brisk walk.'

'In Kensington Gardens?'

'I leave the venue to you.'

'I wasn't asking your opinion, I was asking you to join me. To make sure I do as I'm told.'

It was almost irresistible. Yesterday's cold, driving rain had cleared to one of those perfect late-autumn days. Clear and bright with an eggshell-blue sky. In the park the branches would be bare, but russet leaves would be heaped up and I could almost feel my hand clasped in his as we kicked them up like a couple of kids.

I was clearly losing my mind.

'I'm sure you're a man of your word,' I said discouragingly, and finally handed him the salt. 'Besides, I have to shop for a new suit so that I'll look good on Monday.'

'For the new job?'

'For the new job,' I confirmed. 'In fact, I need a whole new wardrobe of working clothes.'

'Tell me about it.'

He wanted to know about my clothes? Don never noticed what I was wearing. Don wasn't gay, I reminded myself. Even so, he never made me feel quite this...physical.

'Okay. Let's see. I'm going to need a minimum of two suits, four tops...' I was working on the same basic principle as the winter uniform provided by the bank.

'The job,' he said, stopping me before it got any more personal.

'What?'

'Tell me about the job.'

Idiot. Fool. Nincompoop. Just because he was... I

stopped. I still couldn't credit it, Cal exuded the kind
of sexual masculinity that turned heads. Even in this
crowded little restaurant I was aware of surreptitious
glances from other women. Whatever it was that Kate
could see in him, it couldn't be *that* obvious. Which
made me feel a little better. But not much. It wasn't
only women who were looking in our direction.

But that was beside the point. I'd been thinking in
stereotypes. Why would he be in the least bit interested in my wardrobe?

'I'm on temporary secondment,' I said, moving
swiftly on. And I told him the name of the merchant
bank in the City where I had to present myself first
thing on Monday morning.

He frowned. 'I thought you said you worked in a
high street bank.'

'I do. Did.' Then, realising he assumed I was a
counter clerk, 'I'm an FPC. A financial planning con-
sultant. Pensions, investments…'

'Oh, I see.'

I'd have had to be a saint not to have enjoyed the
moment when he realised I wasn't quite as stupid as
I looked. But I just said, 'I still have to wear a uniform. It's hardly high fashion…' it made me look
nearer thirty-two than twenty-two, but that was probably the intention; in the Shires people preferred a
little gravitas in their investment advisers '…but it
made life easy. Now I have to start from scratch.' I
shrugged. 'And to be honest I don't know where to
begin.'

'Why don't you ask those girls you're sharing with

to help? They'll be able to point you in the direction of the right places to shop.'

I didn't doubt it. I'd seen the kind of clothes they wore and, no question, they'd got shopping down to an art form.

'Kate, maybe. Sophie…' I pulled a face. 'Putting myself in Sophie's hands does not seem like a sound idea. Besides,' I said, 'with my hair, making an impression is not an option.'

He grinned. 'You're certainly difficult to ignore.'

'That's not a compliment, is it?'

'I guess that depends on whether you want to be a stand-out-in-the-crowd head turner, or prefer to keep a low profile.'

'Tiger or mouse,' I said, more to myself than to Cal.

'Tiger, no argument,' he said. 'I've never seen a mouse with your colouring.'

I dragged both hands over my hair to flatten it against my head. It had been a personal agony from the day I'd been old enough to look in a mirror and realised that, unlike my siblings, I'd inherited my father's ginger frizz rather than my mother's sleek blonde locks, the kind that seemed to just leap into a perfectly coiled French pleat.

I'd tried to copy her style, skewering my hair in place with pins before plastering it down with superhold hair spray. I'd got as far as my desk before it had exploded, showering the office with shrapnel.

'I tried cutting it once,' I told him, 'hoping that, if there was less of it, it wouldn't be so noticeable. I just looked like a ginger poodle.' I'd hoped that by making Cal laugh, I might crack the tension that was holding us together in a force field, excluding everyone else in the café. I didn't get so much as a flicker from him. 'I even tried dyeing it black,' I said, a touch desperately. 'I had to live with the curious greenish tinge for months which, let me tell you, is no joke when you're a teenager.'

He reached up, took hold of my wrists and drew them towards his chest. 'Listen to me, Philly. Your hair is magnificent. Beautiful.' His hands slid over mine and he held them in his. 'The gaze of every man in this place has been riveted on you since we arrived. If I were to reach out, touch your hair—' he let go of one of my hands, reached out and captured a tiny corkscrew curl, stretching it out until it was quite straight before letting it go so that it bounced back, making me jump '—I'd be the most envied man in the room.'

He raised a brow in an invitation to look around, check it out for myself, but I wasn't looking anywhere but at him. And I didn't give him an argument. I didn't have any breath left to spare.

'Your Don should never have let you out of his sight if he wants to keep you,' he said. 'And you can tell him that I said so.' Then, as if slightly embarrassed by the intensity with which he'd spoken, he released my hand and sat back in his chair. 'As for clothes,' he said, in a throwaway manner, 'asking Sophie's advice is probably the quickest way to turn her from disgruntled flatmate into friend. Tell her that you have no idea where to shop—'

'I haven't.'

'Appeal to her good taste and she won't be able to resist the challenge.'

The challenge? I glanced down at my jacket, the expensive silk scarf, which, far from lending style and elegance to my appearance, was trailing in my break-fast. I rescued it and blotted it with a paper napkin.

'My attempt at casual chic didn't impress you, huh?' I said, with what I hoped was a wry grin. It felt more like a grimace.

He returned a smile that was an essay in 'wry'; a demonstration of how it should be done. 'Was I sup-posed to be impressed?'

Oh, hell! If he were straight, we'd be flirting. But since he wasn't, I suppose it didn't much matter. 'Hell, yes,' I said.

'You look exactly right for a wander around a street market on a Saturday morning and I—'

I waited for him to finish, but he chose discretion. I wasn't having that. We were friends. 'But?' I prompted.

'But nothing,' he said, a little tersely. 'This isn't about your dress sense. It's about having to share a flat with Sophie Harrington for six months. From ev-erything I've heard about her, she lives to shop. Challenge her to make you look a million dollars on a budget and she'll break her neck to show you just how good she is.'

'I think perhaps "a million dollars" is expecting

rather too much,' I said, looking down at my watch so that he wouldn't be able to read what must be clearly written in my face. That there was only one pair of eyes I wanted riveted on me. 'But I should be getting back soon. If you've finished?' Neither of us had done justice to breakfast, but he nodded.

I reached for the bill. I always shared expenses with Don, but Cal had already beaten me to the ticket machine at the underground. Bought me an expensive book. Breakfast was my shout.

But he put his hand on the bill before I could take it and forestalled any protest with a look that said 'don't even think about it'.

Since I'd already opened my mouth I had to say something. I said, 'Thank you.'

Some tiger.

CHAPTER SIX

You're writing home to your boyfriend about your new life and friends in London. How much are you going to tell him?

a. everything. He's told you he wants to know how you're spending every minute of the day without him. How sweet.

b. everything that will interest him. Since you haven't been to a football match, it will be a short letter.

c. everything that will make him smile. Just the zany little anecdotes that will make him remember why he loves you.

d. everything—except that you're spending a lot of time with the dishy man who lives next door.

e. everything you can fit on a postcard. You're having too much fun to waste time writing letters.

'WHAT about this?' Cal held up a bowl. 'It's about the right size, it's got the same maker's mark and the colours look about right.'

'It's hopeless. I haven't got a clue what the wretched bowl looked like.' To be brutally honest, I hadn't even noticed it before it had smashed at my feet and, by the time Cal had walked over it, the pieces were too small to provide more than a sketchy idea of the pattern.

'Philly,' he said gently. 'Don't fret. The flat was undoubtedly furnished by a decorator and I doubt that anyone could swear exactly what that bowl looked like.' Then he grinned. 'Except perhaps the cleaner who dusts around it once a week.'

'Do you think so?' I asked doubtfully. Our home was filled with treasures gathered during my parents' long and happy marriage. Everything was known and loved by my mother, from her precious collection of old plates to our infant-school efforts at pottery. Every chip or crack had a story.

To choose to live in surroundings designed by someone else, furnished by a stranger, was beyond imagining.

'Really.' Cal smiled reassuringly.

'You're right. I'm being a pain and you're being very patient.' I turned to the assistant who'd been hovering hopefully. 'How much is this?' I asked. She named a price that wasn't quite as horrendous as I'd anticipated, but before I could say 'wrap it' Cal responded with a counter bid. There was some good-natured haggling and I suspected that his green eyes and a smile that could melt permafrost did more to knock the price down than any suggestion that it might be a touch over-priced.

Or maybe I was biased. For a smile like that, I'd have *given* him the wretched bowl, I thought as I stowed it carefully in my carrier, along with the book he'd bought me.

'I don't know how to thank you. You've been...'
I was going to say 'wonderful', but realised just in
time that it sounded a bit gushing for mere friendship
and I made one of those gestures that suggested I
couldn't have done it without him. Which wasn't totally true. I'd have stressed a whole lot more and paid
a little more, but I'd have managed. It had, however,
been a whole lot more fun doing it with him.

'Now you have to help me choose a peace-offering
for Jay,' he said, taking my arm and leading me out
of the arcade and into the street. The sun was still
shining, gleaming off copper pots and piled high trin-
kets on the street stalls. On the corner of the street
the band was playing 'Jingle Bells', but just the mention of Jay's name took the glow out of the day.
'There's a place that sells walking sticks and umbrellas in that gallery over there.'

I kept forgetting about Jay. Every time Cal looked
at me, or touched me, or said something in that soft,
gravelly voice.

My brain—the rational, thinking part of me—knew
none of it meant anything. For some reason, the responsive, feeling part of me refused to cotton on.

I knew I had no right to be feeling...whatever it
was I was feeling. Okay, I was fudging, here. Just
because the feeling was new and unexpected didn't
mean I didn't recognise it.

But I had no right to be feeling jealous of Jay. Any
more than Don should feel jealous of Cal.

He was a friend. He was safe.

And if my insides melted like toasted marshmallow

when he looked at me, when he touched my hair, well, I wasn't going to shout it from the rooftops and make a total fool of myself, was I?

Cal stopped by one of the street stalls. It was packed with interesting old tools. 'Do you want to look for something for Don?'

'Don?'

He glanced down at me. 'Just a little something to reassure him that he's in your thoughts,' he said, picking up a fine brass metalworking gauge. And I had the uneasy feeling that he was testing me. That he knew Don hadn't troubled my thoughts all morning. 'Old tools are very collectible.'

'Are they?' My voice came out as little more than a croak.

Whatever was the matter with me? Worse than not giving Don a thought, I hadn't even phoned him. My last words had been to reassure him that it was all right, that I understood why he hadn't been able to come to the station with me. That I'd call him to let him know I'd arrived safely.

At the time I'd meant it, but actually I didn't understand and it wasn't 'all right'. The tiger in me was more than a little tired of coming third in his life. After his car. And his mother.

'It won't do him any harm to worry about that for a day or two,' I said, rather shocking myself. For a moment I froze. But the sky didn't fall in. The world continued to turn. Cal was still smiling despite the fact that I'd just betrayed myself as the kind of girl-

friend who'd make the man in her life sweat. 'I'll
send him a postcard from the Science Museum.'

'Wish you were here?'

'Enough of Don,' I said. 'We have to give Jay our
undivided attention right now.' And I took the brass
gauge Cal was offering me and returned it to the stall
without even looking at it. 'I got the very strong impression that if you upset him, he might just chop
your film into tiny little bits.'

Cal laughed. Really laughed so that several people
turned to look. One, a tall and teeth-gnashingly lovely
brunette, lingered beside the stall as if interested in
an old spanner. And how likely was that?

Before she could play the helpless female and gain
his attention by asking for his advice, I tucked my
arm possessively through his and raised a 'get lost'
eyebrow in her direction. She blinked, then gave me
a you-can't-blame-a-girl-for-trying shrug.

'Am I right?' I asked, turning Cal in the direction
of the gallery before he could notice her. Not that it
mattered. But still… 'Or am I right?'

'No dispute,' he said, still grinning. 'But Jay's an
artist. Temperament comes as standard.'

'Rubbish. He's just a drama queen—' I caught myself, swallowed, but Cal didn't look offended. On the
contrary, he looked as if he was finding it hard not to
laugh out loud. Encouraged, I went on. 'The only reason he has something to work on is because you spent
months up to your neck in elephant dung fighting off
mosquitoes the size of bats.'

'Very small bats,' he said, removing his arm from

mine and placing it at my back to ease me through the crowds, but as I stopped at the door to the tiny umbrella shop he caught my arm, holding me in the entrance, and I looked up. He was still smiling, but there was a look in his eyes as if he was seeing something else. Something a long way from the teeming mass of bargain hunters seeking out unusual Christmas gifts.

'There's a moment on the Serengeti, Philly, just as dawn breaks and the watering hole turns to liquid gold when you're looking at the world as it was ten thousand years ago. It's worth any amount of discomfort, any amount of pain just to be there.' The intensity of the moment made me shiver suddenly. Cal saw it and rubbed his hand comfortingly up and down my arm. 'No matter how brilliantly Jay edits the film, no matter how many awards are heaped on his head and mine as a result of his work, he only ever sees it second hand. He never gets to experience the reality.'

Like me? For a moment it seemed that he was trying to show me that I'd been viewing life, living life, through a net curtain.

Clearly the red wine had scrambled my brain cells. 'All the pleasure, none of the discomfort,' I said, with forced brightness. 'Sounds good to me.' Well, I was the archetypal armchair traveller.

'Does it?' And then he was back with me, giving me his undivided attention. Looking at me as if he wasn't convinced and ignoring the crowds pushing past us, he said, 'Close your eyes.'

'But—'

'Close your eyes.' There was an urgency about him, a sudden intensity that was impossible to ignore, and I closed my eyes. 'Imagine you're sitting on a sofa, warm and comfortable in front of the fire watching film of a stormy sea breaking against a rocky coastline. Got that?'

I nodded. 'Got it.' It didn't need much imagination. The sofa and I were old friends. Only the man I was sharing it with, snuggled up to in the dark, was different.

'Now imagine standing on the cliff top, feeling the thud of it beneath your feet as it smashes against the rocks a hundred feet below, smelling wind that's crossed a thousand miles of ocean, tasting the salt spray on your lips.' He paused for a moment, giving me time to imagine the scene, feel it. 'How do you feel now, Philly?'

'Cold,' I offered. 'Wet.'

Alive.

It was as if I'd been feeling in monochrome and without warning Cal had tuned me into full colour. But if I said that, it was admitting that until I'd met him I'd been jogging along with my senses on a pilot light. And if I admitted that what did it say about me? About my life?

About what he was doing to me?

Way too much.

'Is that all?'

'What else?' I asked as I opened my eyes. And shivered again, this time intentionally, before stepping into the shop.

He didn't pursue it, although I sensed he wasn't entirely convinced, instead he turned to the beautifully made old umbrellas, taking way too long, in my opinion, to choose one. What was to choose? They were all black. But he seemed in no hurry and I wasn't in any hurry for the morning to end. The net curtain had been raised, my senses had been switched on and I was in no rush to return to the person I'd been.

He finally narrowed it down to two.

'Which do you prefer?'

I took them from him, but I couldn't see much difference between them. 'Why don't you buy both?' I suggested. 'Jay could choose the one he likes best and you could keep the other for yourself.' I just hated the idea of him borrowing Jay's again. Stupid or what?

'No, thanks. They're nothing but trouble. The only kind of umbrella I use is one of those big golf umbrellas to keep the equipment dry.'

'Oh, right. Well, in that case, I think we should go with this one,' I said, squinting at the tag, trying not to wince as I handed it to the dealer, and, being a quick learner, putting myself between him and Cal until I'd handed over the cash.

'Philly…'

'Cal?' I said, in my most tigerish manner.

'Are you going to be difficult about this?'

'Infinitely,' I said. 'Besides, you haven't got time to argue. You're in enough trouble without being late. And I have to shop.'

He took the umbrella. 'First, we walk.'

'No. Really. I was kidding. You don't look as if you're short of exercise.'

'I'm not, but it's a lovely day and Jay's studio is on the other side of the park. I'll put you in a taxi home when we get there.'

'I could go down the road and get on the underground. It'd be cheaper and probably quicker.'

It wasn't that I was reluctant to walk through the park with him. I was afraid that I wanted to rather too much.

'Of course you could. But I'd be a lot happier knowing that you were going straight back to base rather than wandering about the underground system, not knowing your north from your south.'

'How will I learn if I don't practise?'

'If you insist on the underground I'll have to come with you for my own peace of mind.'

'But you'll be late,' I protested.

'The fate of my film is in your hands.'

'You're going to be difficult about this, aren't you?' I said.

'Infinitely,' he replied, his eyes creasing in the kind of smile that made my knees buckle.

Fool, fool, fool. 'In that case, let's walk.'

As we reached the park he extended his elbow so that I could slip my arm through his and we walked together along the path, not scuffing up the leaves, though, because they were still clumped together in sodden lumps following the rain.

Don wasn't much of an arm-in-arm sort of man.

Being seen that close in public would have embarrassed him. Tucked in against the warmth of Cal's body, I discovered just how much I'd yearned for this kind of warmth, closeness.

Walking arm-in-arm with Cal, I felt…cherished.

And, because I was enjoying it so much, guilty.

'Tell me some more about your work,' I said, trying to distract myself from such disturbing thoughts. 'How does one become a wild-life film-maker?'

He smiled. 'I can only tell you how I became one.' Well, that was all I wanted to know. 'I was having trouble with low-light filming and I wrote to a cameraman whose name appeared on the credits of a film I'd seen on the television. I explained the effects I was trying to achieve and sent him what I'd actually got so that he could see what I was doing wrong. I hoped he'd give me some advice. Instead he invited me along to the studios to see for myself. I knew my parents would say no, so I didn't tell them. Just bunked off school.'

'School? How old were you?'

'Thirteen.'

'That's a bit early to start on a career, isn't it?'

'It wasn't ever meant to be a career, Philly. I was supposed to go to college, qualify as an architect and join the family firm. It was something I did—do—for my own pleasure.'

I thought about the predictability of my own desk-bound job and said, 'There's something vaguely indecent about being paid to do something that you'd happily do for the love of it.'

'Is there? That could be why my family refuse to take it seriously as a career.'

'They don't?' But even as I said it I remembered how, when I'd said how proud his mother must be, he'd said, 'Must she?'

'They don't.' Then, 'Your turn.'

'For what?'

'Secrets. You don't think I'd tell just anyone that my family disapproves of me, do you?'

'Well, no.'

'So, tell me something about yourself that you've never told anyone else.'

I glanced at him, not sure how to take that, but he just lifted his eyebrows encouragingly. 'There isn't anything. I'm an open book,' I said. And then blushed. Because of course there was something. But I couldn't... 'Well, I'm really, really scared of spiders,' I said. I had to say something.

'And you've managed to keep that a secret?' He knew I was hiding the real secret, but he played along with me. 'How? Do you have a special quiet scream that no one can hear?'

'No, really, it's true. I pretend. I've been pretending all my life. When you've got three big brothers who'll exploit any weakness, do anything to make you scream, you must never let them see that you're afraid. Even when they put them in your bed, then hang about on the landing waiting for you to let rip.'

'Oh, charming.'

'Spider in the bath? I just scoop it out of the window as if I'm not in the least bit concerned. And then

I take a shower...' Just talking about it made me shiver and Cal put his arm around me.

'If you find any spiders while you're living next door to me, just come and get me.'

'My hero,' I said, and laughed.

'And you can tell me the other secret, the one that made you blush, when you know me better.' He didn't wait for my protest, but stopped to watch a grey squirrel hurtling around the trunk of a tall tree.

'You're going to be late,' I warned him.

'I know.' But he didn't hurry.

'Tell me some more about Africa,' I said. 'The cheetahs. When is your film going to be shown on television?'

He began to talk about what he'd seen, the horrors, the wonders, unimaginable beauty, so that I lost all sense of time until he took his arm from my shoulders, raising his hand to hail a cruising taxi. I looked around in surprise to discover that we'd reached the far side of the park, then at my watch. It was nearly half-past one.

'Oh, good grief, look at the time!'

'Don't worry about it. Have you got a mobile phone?' he said.

'What? Oh, yes.' He raised his eyebrows for the number and I rattled it off. He didn't write it down, but he'd taken out a card with his name and number on it.

'This is mine. If you have any problems,' he said, opening the taxi door, 'if you get lost—need help with anything—call me.'

'Problems? Me?' I said, laughing, letting go the feeling that I'd just come close to the heart of Callum McBride. 'What can you mean?' But I took the card and tucked it safely in my bag feeling—well, there was only one word for it—cherished all over again. Then as I climbed aboard he spoke to the driver, giving him the address of the apartment and money to cover the fare.

I didn't waste my breath protesting, but leaned forward in the seat. 'Thank you for today, Cal. And yesterday. I don't know what I'd have done without you.'

'You'd have coped.' And he touched his lips to my cold cheek. Then, 'I'll see you later,' he said almost abruptly, stepping back and shutting the door.

I was still feeling the roughness of his stubble as the taxi pulled away from the kerb and I twisted in my seat to look back out of the window. Still drowning in a complex combination of scents that clung to me and gave meaning to that old phrase 'I'll never wash that cheek again'. Still wallowing in that promise of 'later'.

But Cal wasn't following the cab with his gaze. His eyes were already lifted to a window opposite, high above street-level, his hand raised to acknowledge Jay who, impatient for his arrival, was looking out for him.

The reality of that look, the responsive wave, hit me like a fist and the air rushed out of me in a grunt of pain as real as if the assault had been physical, rather than emotional.

'Did you say something, miss?'

'What?' I couldn't speak. I could hardly breathe. Then, hugging myself around the waist, I said, 'The Science Museum is near here, isn't it? Will you take me there, please?'

He glanced back at me. 'The gent paid me to take you all the way to Chelsea.' He clearly didn't relish giving up the fare.

'I don't care about the money. Keep it. I just want to go to the Science Museum.' I'd been away from Maybridge for less than twenty-four hours and it seemed unreal, no longer part of my life. I had to remind myself what was really important to me. Not London, not Cal, but Don and the life we'd—I'd—been planning for us for so long.

Sophie and Kate were sitting in the kitchen, the remains of breakfast littering the work surfaces, a pot of coffee steaming gently on the breakfast bar. 'The electrics are back in full working order, then?' I said, putting the porcelain bowl I'd purchased in front of Kate and, at her unspoken invitation, pouring myself a cup of coffee.

'Electrics?' she said.

'I blew the fuses when I tried to use the grill last night. I left an electrician sorting it out this morning.'

Kate turned on Sophie. 'You said you'd dealt with that!'

'I did,' Sophie said, glaring at me as if I were the school snitch. 'I stuck a note on the cooker point saying "Do Not Use".' Then, when the silence grew too long to ignore, 'I suppose it must have fallen off. Sorry,' she muttered.

'No harm done,' I said, intervening quickly before Kate exploded. 'I fixed the fuse with a little help from the man at number seventy-two…' I had no intention of explaining how much time I'd spent with him '…and he kindly organised an electrician to fix the stove.'

'He's such a sweetie,' Kate agreed. 'It's a shame he's leaving.'

'Leaving?' Communing with the assembly-line-perfect twin of Don's beloved 1922 Austin on display in the Science Museum hadn't prepared me for the shock of hearing that news. 'When?'

Kate frowned. 'It must be soon. He told me two or three weeks ago. I don't know, time flies. He doesn't own the place, he just leased it temporarily.'

'Oh, I see. He didn't mention that he was leaving.' But of course it was obvious he wouldn't need a permanent base when he was away so much. Plans for his turtle expedition must be rather more advanced than he'd implied. 'The thing is,' I said, preferring not to comment on whether it was a shame or not he was leaving. Eager to change the subject altogether, in fact. 'Last night, in the dark, I managed to break a bowl. So I bought this.' And I unwrapped it and offered it to Kate. 'I know it can't replace the original, but I hope your aunt won't be too cross.'

'Oh, Philly, you didn't have to do that.' She looked up. 'Aunt Cora would have understood, but Sophie will have to refund you, since the whole incident was her fault.'

Sophie's scowl instantly deepened and I said, 'No!' And, 'That really isn't necessary, Sophie. But I was sort of hoping that you would do something for me. A favour. Instead,' I added, just to make it clear that I was not expecting to be reimbursed for the bowl.

She looked at me with all the suspicion of a cat regarding a fresh fall of snow. 'What kind of favour?'

I restrained the urge to slap her and instead gave a helpless little shrug. 'The thing is, I need some clothes.' Then, 'Well, a whole new work wardrobe, to be honest. I haven't got a clue where to start. What I should buy. The best shops…'

'This is urgent?' she said, brightening considerably at the prospect, but still persisting in making it sound like a real pain. Out of the corner of my eye I saw Kate grin and nod, very slightly, as she acknowledged my tactics to win her sister over.

'I'm afraid it is, rather. Is it an awful imposition?' I didn't give her a chance to answer that. 'The thing is, I start a new job on Monday morning and I'm panicking that I'll look like a country cousin.' Her eyes, over the rim of her coffee-cup, suggested that I would always look like a country cousin. 'I wore a uniform at the building society. Maybe I should just get something similar,' I said. 'Navy blue, red piping, blouse with a pussycat bow?' Sophie, spluttering, was sufficient repayment for having to grovel. 'It's very neat,' I said, beginning to enjoy myself. 'I suppose the girls will wear something similar at this merchant bank place?'

'What merchant bank place?' I told her and she was off her stool and through the door before I could blink. 'Just give me ten minutes,' she called back as she headed for her room.

'That was absolutely wicked,' Kate said, finally able to let herself go and laugh. Quietly. 'Have you really got a job at Bartlett's?'

'I've been seconded to cover maternity leave. As a favour between bank executives.' Among other things. 'It's only temporary.'

'That doesn't matter. With access to all those upwardly mobile high-earning young bankers Sophie will be your new best friend.'

That was rather more than I'd looked for, but it had to be better than the alternative. 'Great,' I said.

My mobile beeped, warning me that I had a text message. I took it out of my bag and turned it on. 'Umbrella total success. Home safe? C.'

I didn't want to know that Jay was happy and, ignoring Cal's concern for my safety, I flipped my phone shut again. When I looked up I realised Kate was looking at me with that I-won't-ask-but-it's-killing-me expression. 'It's nothing,' I said, and felt my cheeks heat up. 'Just a friend. I'll call back later.'

'Sure,' Kate said.

It was obvious that she didn't believe me. To be honest, I didn't quite believe it myself. I had no idea how Cal would describe our relationship, but I knew I was way beyond 'just a friend'.

'Oh, bother, I should have told you before, Philly. There was a call for you while you were out.'

'Don?' I asked, a panicky feeling of guilt welling up in me like a flood. I couldn't speak to Don right now, not with my head stuffed with thoughts and feelings I didn't understand.

'Your mother,' Kate said. 'What a sweet woman. She said it was some dreadful time in the middle of the night, but she couldn't sleep so she thought she'd call to let you know that she and your father have arrived safely.'

'Oh, right. Thanks.'

'Who's Don?'

'What?'

'You thought the call was from someone called Don.'

'Oh, yes.' I pulled a comic face to cover my confused feelings. 'He's the boy next door,' I said.

'Sweet,' she said.

At this point I usually told the entire story. How we met. The bicycle. How we intended to spend the rest of our lives together in lovely Maybridge. None of that seemed quite real any more, so I just smiled and said, 'Yes, he is.'

Then assuaged my conscience by getting out the postcard I'd bought at the museum—a picture of the baby Austin, 'motor for the millions'—and quickly wrote, 'Wish you were here,' in the message space.

Then I changed the full stop to a question mark. The truth was, right at that moment I didn't really want Don 'here'.

What I wanted was some space to work out exactly where our relationship was going and 'Wish you were here?' had an entirely different meaning.

One I was a lot more comfortable with.

CHAPTER SEVEN

*Your best friend asks you to make up a foursome
with a man you're 'going to adore on sight'. Do
you:*

*a. leap at the chance? Nothing ventured, nothing
gained. Her boyfriend is captain of the local rugby
team and all his mates have to be hunks, right?*

*b. remember the last time with a barely sup-
pressed shudder, but, hey, it couldn't possibly be
that bad again?*

*c. tell her, without excuses, that you don't do
blind dates?*

*d. remind her that you have a boyfriend back
home…and ignore her laughter?*

*e. when she won't take no for an answer, 'text' a
friend to call with some imaginary crisis?*

'PHILLY?'

I was shattered. Broke and shattered. Sophie had
shopped till I dropped. It was just as well that Don
wasn't panting for a wedding—I'd just blown my
trousseau savings on a new wardrobe.

I suspected the fact that this didn't seem to matter
should have bothered me a lot more than it did.

Sophie, however, had apparently been supercharged by the thrill of buying clothes on someone else's credit card. While I'd slumped in an armchair, she'd curled up kitten-like, a glass of wine in one hand, my magazine in the other, and was giggling at the tiger/mouse quiz she'd discovered while she was supposed to be helping me put away my new clothes. She'd reached the 'blind date' question and wasn't taking 'shut up' as an answer.

'Come on, Philly, take a risk,' she encouraged. 'You can't possibly be as sweet and mouse-like as you look. Not with your colouring.'

'I can't?' Cal had said much the same thing as he'd played with my hair. Just thinking about his fingers curling through it, his knuckles brushing against my cheek, made my skin prickle.

He'd sent two more text messages, the second a slightly anxious—''Philly, where are you?'' The third a simple demand— ''Call me!''

I wanted to, heaven knew. Wanted to call him. Wanted to hear his voice. Be close enough to him for my senses to be charged with the scent of his skin. Feel his cool lips against my skin…

'Hello-o-o? Are you with me?'

'What? Oh, yes,' I lied. I wasn't even in the same room. I was sitting in a café having breakfast with Cal, his fingers on mine. In the park, tucked up close against him, my hand on the soft rubbed leather of his jacket, walking through soggy leaves. In a taxi, shivering at the touch of his jaw against my skin as he'd kissed my cheek, lingering just long enough to give me ideas…

I wanted to call him so much. Wanted his voice grating softly against my ear…

I realised Sophie was looking at me a little oddly and I pulled myself together. 'I'm thinking,' I said.

'It's a quiz in a magazine, Philly. Not Mastermind.'

No, and twenty-four hours ago I wouldn't have thought twice about the answer. I'd have immediately plumped for 'e'. I had a boyfriend back home. But Don had faded from my mind like a photograph left out in the sun. All I wanted to do was switch on my mobile and check to see if there was another text message from Cal.

All that stopped me was the way he'd looked up at the window where Jay had been waiting for him. He might be thinking about me. Worrying about me. But he was with Jay.

'Put her down for the boyfriend back home.' Kate, stretched out flat on the sofa with a pair of cold tea bags over her eyes in preparation for another big night with her barrister, was clearly tired of the whole thing. 'She's going to marry the boy next door.'

'Are you?' Sophie asked, unflatteringly astonished. 'I mean actually engaged, or anything? You're not wearing a ring.'

No, I wasn't. Not engaged. Not even 'anything'. And remembering my determination to turn my life around, become a tiger, I said, 'To be honest, the boy next door is more interested in his car than in me.'

I'd meant it as a joke, but as I said the words I realised that it wasn't remotely funny, it was true. I'd devoted years of my life to Don while he'd devoted his to an unending line of decrepit vehicles. Infatuated from the first moment I'd set eyes on him, I was the dream girlfriend. Never demanding, always there— he'd never had to make the slightest effort to hold my attention. Okay, so that wasn't his fault, it was mine. But, put to the test, he still hadn't bothered.

'Maybe you should put me down as an "a",' I said, with a mirthless grin.

Kate, startled, lost the tea bags as she turned to look at me. Sophie, missing the irony, grinned right back. 'Excellent choice,' she said. 'You've got an hour to get ready. Wear something sexy. Tony adores cuddly girls with lots of hair and minimal clothes.'

What?

Minimal clothes?

Whoa!

'Tony? Who's Tony?' I asked, overlooking the 'cuddly' as my bravado collapsed in a huddle and the 'tiger' in me bypassed kitten and turned into pure mouse.

'He's just a friend. Nice bloke. You'll like him.'

'Nice!' Kate covered her face with her hands and groaned. 'I thought you were a safe "e", Philly, or I'd have warned you. For future reference the only other answer to that question is option "d".' *You do not do blind dates.*'

Consumed with relief at being rescued from my own stupidity—I appeared to have left my brain behind when I'd packed—I managed a laugh. 'Well, actually, no, I don't—'

'Tony is fun,' Sophie cut in.

'Yeah, right. That's why the only dates he ever gets are blind ones.'

'Okay, I'll admit he's a bit *boisterous*—' for a moment they appeared to forget I was there '—when he's had a few drinks. But he's a really, really nice guy beneath it all. Shy, even.'

'Oh, please!'

'Actually…' I repeated and they both turned to me. 'I don't have anything sexy to wear.' Fortunately, Sophie had been single-minded in her pursuit of the perfect business suit and, despite the tempting displays of Christmas party clothes, had refused to be distracted by anything remotely frivolous. 'I didn't really plan on…um…dating—'

As I said the word, it occurred to me that I'd never actually been out on a date. What did you do? What did you talk about? Don's favourite topic of conversation was the Austin's bodywork. With a 'minimal clothes' dress code, it seemed likely that Tony's interest in bodywork would be rather more personal.

If it had been Cal I'd have had no problems. Talking was easy. So was silence. And he could get as personal as he liked…

Did I say I was a fool? Triple that.

Fool, fool, fool.

'Oh, it's not a *date*,' Sophie said quickly. 'There'll be a crowd of us and you can't spend your first Saturday night in London on your own.' My face must have betrayed my doubts because she rushed on, 'Don't worry about clothes. We'll fix you up with something. And you can give those delicious high heels you bought a trial run.'

I interpreted that as, 'I spent my afternoon helping you out. It's time to return the favour.'

'But…' About to say that I wasn't planning on having a good time, I realised just how wet that would sound. It *was* Saturday night and Don would be down the pub with the rest of the gang. I trusted him—no one knew better than me just how trustworthy he was—but he was a good-looking guy and there wouldn't be any shortage of girls eager to make sure he wasn't lonely. Realising that Sophie and Kate were waiting for me to finish, I shook my head. 'Nothing,' I said. Then swallowed. Hard.

An hour later I was standing in my room wearing next-to-nothing in black that had been made for someone a lot less 'cuddly' than me and a pair of four-inch heels that Sophie had insisted were a 'must' to complete my sharp new City-girl image. Absolutely *me*.

My reflection didn't look like any 'me' that I recognised.

I tugged on the stretch-fabric of the dress in an attempt to cover another inch of traffic-stopping bosom. I didn't dare tug at the hem. The dress was only staying put by the snugness of fit and pure willpower. Tony was going to take one look at me and think Christmas had come a month early.

And I was the turkey.

All that was missing was a pair of flashing 'Santa' earrings.

I had three options. One, I could beef up my outfit with a smile and go along with Sophie's idea of a good time in the interests of promoting flat-sharing harmony. Tony's idea was something else.

Two, since he liked girls with 'lots of hair', I could take a pair of scissors to mine. It wasn't as if I were deeply attached to it. At least, I hadn't been until Cal had twisted it around his fingers and told me it was beautiful…

Was that why I'd gone to so much trouble, plastering on the conditioner so that the frizz had been smoothed out into tiny curls? Because we might meet in the hall…share the lift…

I dismissed the idea as ridiculous. I wasn't thinking about Cal. Why would I care what he thought? He didn't care about me. He just thought I was a stupid girl who couldn't stay out of trouble for five minutes. Couldn't manage a simple taxi ride without someone to hold my hand.

My fingers bunched into a fist as if to fend off the memory of his palm against mine.

He hadn't even bothered to tell me he was moving out. Imminently. The way he'd talked about the turtle project, I'd assumed it was months away.

I made a determined effort to ignore the hollow feeling in the pit of my stomach. I had more immediate problems.

Three options? Oh, right. I could try the final choice in the quiz and use my mobile to phone a friend to bail me out. Unfortunately, since there was only one other person I knew in London—and I'd not only strained his Galahad potential to the limit but had been ignoring his messages all afternoon—that was a non-starter.

'The taxi's here,' Sophie said, putting her head around the door. 'Are you ready?' Then, 'Wow! You look totally knockout. Tony won't believe his luck when I turn up with you!'

'He'd better not get too excited,' I said. Ready. And right out of options.

I picked up the long and supremely elegant black coat I'd bought that afternoon. It had seemed an incredible extravagance at the time, but at least it would keep me covered from neck to ankle. I might not take it off all night.

Sophie, anxious to go, hustled me out of the flat before I could put it on and punched the button to summon the lift.

I had an arm through one sleeve as the doors slid back to reveal Cal. He looked tired and irritable and there was a moment of total silence as he took in my appearance. 'My god, Philly...' he finally managed.

I tried to speak but my mouth was glued shut. How did he do it? How did he know when I was in trouble and come racing to my rescue like the Seventh Cavalry?

He stepped from the lift, reached for my hand, holding it away from me so that he could get the whole effect. My expensive new coat slithered to the floor, unnoticed.

'You look...' He apparently couldn't think of the words to express what he thought I looked like, which was perhaps as well. Instead he stepped forward, put his arm around my waist and pulled me hard against his body. The air rushed out of me, leaving me breathless—something was leaving me breathless 'Different,' he said. Then, presumably to stop me from demanding to know in what way 'different', he kissed me. And this time it wasn't on the cheek.

I thought I'd been kissed. Don and I had practised that bit quite extensively—although not much recently, I had to admit—and I was certain I knew all there was to know about kissing. I was wrong.

This was new. Cal's mouth was possessive, passionate, thorough, taking full advantage of the element of surprise.

And with one hand holding me firmly about my waist and the other cradling my head, fingers tangled in my hair, I wasn't going anywhere until he'd finished what he'd started.

That was okay. I wasn't in any hurry for him to stop.

Sophie, though, doubtless mindful of the waiting taxi, eventually cleared her throat pointedly and Cal let me go. At least he raised his head a couple of inches and, while still close enough so that Sophie couldn't see, he raised one eyebrow a fraction. Just enough to let me know that this was indeed no more than the rescue I'd hoped for. And that he hadn't entirely lost his mind.

He was alone there. Mine was nowhere to be found as he finally straightened, releasing my head but still keeping a firm grip on my waist as he said, 'You can't possibly go out like that.'

'I can't?'

Yes!

'Not unless I'm there to take care of you.'

'You're more than welcome to join us,' Sophie said quickly.

'Thanks, but it's been a long day.' And keeping his arm firmly about my waist, he turned to face her. 'But if that's your taxi downstairs, I have to tell you that the driver is getting impatient.'

'Oops! I must run.'

'I'm sorry,' I said, turning to Sophie with reluctance, anticipating major irritation at having her captive 'blind date' hijacked in this fashion, but she was grinning broadly.

'Crumbs, Philly,' she said. 'Don't apologise. I was sure you were going to be the world's most boring flatmate. I mean, any girl who's still living at home at your age would have to be, right?'

Right.

She gave Cal an appreciative look. 'But I have to admit that in your shoes I wouldn't have been in any hurry to leave home, either.' And with that, she stepped into the lift. 'I'd say have fun,' she said, reaching for the ground-floor button, 'but it's clear that you don't need any encouragement.'

'What will you tell Tony?' I asked, stopping the lift door as it began to close. My conscience getting the better of common sense.

'Absolutely nothing. I was keeping you as a sur-

prise and I'm not going to break his heart by telling
him how near he came to meeting the girl of his
dreams.'

I felt Cal's hand tighten at my waist as I hesitated.
'You're keeping Miss Harrington from her friends,'
he said, pulling me back. And the doors slid together
leaving me alone with him.

I turned to look back up at him, expecting amusement at another fine mess I'd got myself into. But he
wasn't laughing. Maybe he was angry. I couldn't tell.
His eyes were dark and bottomless and unreadable
and I hadn't the least idea what he was thinking.
Feeling. And he didn't say anything that might give
me a clue.

'How did you know?' I said quickly. Well, I had
to say something to fill that yawning chasm of silence
that was nowhere near as restful as it had been in the
park that morning.

He stirred and until then I hadn't realised how close
we were. How still he'd been. How wonderful it had
been just to stand there with his arm around my waist,
my body wrapped in his warmth.

'Know?' He frowned.

'That I wanted to be rescued? I considered sending
you a text message but—'

'A text message?' Something about the way he said
that warned me it had been a mistake to mention text
messages. 'It's a funny thing about text messages.
I've been trying to get in touch with someone all afternoon but she had her phoned switched off, didn't
pick up her voice mail, and totally ignored her mes-

sages. In the end my battery went flat and I had to come home to check out for myself that she hadn't got lost. Or into trouble, picking up strange men in taxis.'

'Just as well I didn't bother trying to call you, then,' I said, aiming for pertness.

'It's no bother,' he said, not letting go as he stooped to pick up my coat, hand it to me. It was all I could do to stop myself from wrapping it about me to stop him looking at me. His expression was still giving nothing away and yet I had this uneasy feeling that I was Red Riding Hood and he was the wolf.

Instead I clutched it to me as he cupped my cheek in the cool palm of his hand. 'And in answer to your question, Philly,' he said, 'I didn't care whether you wanted to be rescued or not. I just knew that you weren't going anywhere in that dress without me.'

'You mean you…' I made a vague gesture at the black dress that gave a whole new meaning to the word 'little'. 'Then you…' I swallowed as my mind took me on a three-D rerun of the way he'd kissed me.

'That's about it,' he confirmed. I really wished he'd smile… 'Are you angry with me for kissing you?'

'Angry? No! It was absolutely perfect!' And then I strangled a groan, aware that I was in danger of making a complete fool of myself. But the warmth of his mouth, the satiny feel of his tongue against mine, the scent of him that had haunted me all day, had turned on lights inside my head which, until that moment, had only been flickering dimly. Who could think rationally at a moment like that? 'What I mean is—'

'I know what you mean,' he said gently.

I was rather afraid he did. 'Yes, well, thanks again. Maybe one day I'll be able to do the same for you.' Groan, groan, groan. I took a breath and started again. 'I'll rephrase that—'

His mouth didn't change, but the creases at the corner of his eyes finally twitched into the promise of a smile. 'It sounded fine the way it was.'

To which there was no answer. At least, not one that made sense. But none of this was making sense unless he was thinking of Don.

Of course. That had to be it. He was reminding me that I was attached, making sure I didn't do anything that I'd later regret. Looking out for me. Again.

'I'd better go and change into something less traffic-stopping,' I said. And write out a thousand times in my best cursive—I am not a tiger, I never was a tiger and I never will be one. I made a move for the safety of my own front door, but Cal's hand stayed glued to my waist.

'That seems a pity, when you've gone to so much trouble and look so—'

'I know how I look,' I said, before he could say it for me.

'No, Philly. I promise you, you can have absolutely no idea.' And this time his mouth kicked up in the kind of smile that went straight to my knees as, taking my silence for consent, he steered me firmly in the direction of his apartment.

The words frying-pan and fire flashed through my brain.

I dismissed them.

Cal's kiss might have given me a glimpse of everything I'd been missing, possibilities that I'd only dreamed about, but it had been a charade. Nothing but acting for Sophie's benefit. Acting so real, so convincing that it deserved an Oscar. But it was still acting.

I was safe with Cal. Which assuaged my conscience, if nothing else.

'You can show your gratitude by making me a drink while I take a shower,' he said. 'Then we'll go out and get something to eat.'

Safe as houses. Unfortunately. I didn't want to be safe... I wanted to be at serious risk and I wanted Cal to be the source of danger.

'You really don't have to do that,' I said quickly. 'You've done more than enough today and I can't begin to tell you how much I appreciate your help—'

'But?' he said.

But I was getting into something I couldn't handle. Feeling things that under the circumstances were totally inappropriate. He was being kind again. That was all.

And still waiting for an answer. There was nothing I could say so I made one of those vague gestures that meant nothing, that hid what you were really thinking.

Thoughts like, I'd like nothing more than to spend the evening with you—again—but I don't want to be just friends. I want something you can't give me. Something that, until I met you, I hadn't even known existed.

He didn't press me further.

'Then it's me or Tony,' he said as he unlocked his door. 'I'm sure the Harrington girl would come back for you if you gave her a call.'

'What would I tell her? That you decided to kiss and run?' I said, attempting to make a joke of it. Then frowned because something Sophie had said didn't quite make sense. I should have been paying more attention, but under the circumstances... 'I'm not an authority,' I said. 'But it didn't seem to be that kind of kiss.'

'No?' He lost the smile as he stood back to let me go ahead of him. 'Go on through and make yourself at home,' he said, taking my coat, leaving me feeling naked. He hung it up and turned back to me. 'There's some white wine in the fridge.'

'Thanks, but I'll be sticking to mineral water for the foreseeable future.'

'You're a fast learner,' he said, starting on his shirt buttons. Cuffs first, to reveal strong, thick wrists.

I was very quickly learning a whole new set of responses as he started on the front, exposing first his throat, then a sprinkling of dark hair, the flat, tanned flesh of his stomach as he tugged his shirt out of his jeans.

'You?' I said, to distract myself from the revealing way those jeans clung to his hips. From my own rampant imagination.

'I'll have a Scotch. A large one. Straight. On the rocks. It's been that kind of day.'

And it was all my fault. He was my dream neighbour. I had to be his worst nightmare. 'I'm so sorry, Cal.'

'Don't be,' he said, reaching out as if to touch my cheek again, raising the down in eager anticipation, but his fingers curled back against his palm before he made contact. 'Things began to look up the moment the lift doors opened.' And with that he turned abruptly and pushed open a bedroom door. I caught a glimpse of warm terracotta walls, a large creamy bed, before it was shut with rather more force than was usual. As if a sudden weight had been applied to it.

I let out a breath I hadn't been aware of holding— long, steady and slow—before going through to the kitchen for ice, standing in front of the open fridge door for a moment to cool down.

I was hot. Burning where his fingers had touched me. Hot with a longing that was going nowhere. I was the one who should be going, I thought. But I stayed where I was, filling a bowl with ice before carrying it, along with a bottle of mineral water, into the living room.

Cal's apartment was larger than the one I shared with Sophie and Kate, and it was clear that no decorator had had a hand in furnishing it. The windows were tall and bare, giving an unobstructed view of the lights of London, beefed up at this time of year by coloured lights from tall Christmas trees all along the river and holiday lights strung from every possible vantage point.

I'd been trying very hard not to think about Christmas without my family, my friends, Don, and I turned away abruptly to look back at the apartment.

It was totally masculine. Uncluttered. No porcelain frippery here to cause mayhem in the dark. There was an unadorned hole-in-the-wall fireplace with large leather armchairs placed in the comfort zone. Between them a rich Persian rug lay over wide oak boards polished to a warm glow.

Above the fireplace there was a huge black and white photograph, bleached almost white to leave little more than the impression of a tiger in shadows. The signature, Callum McBride, came as no surprise.

What did surprise me was the feeling that this wasn't a temporary home. Everything, furniture, primitive native art that even I could see was the real thing, seemed to fit the man like a well-worn glove.

He might be about to move, but his departure didn't seem imminent. There was certainly nothing to suggest he'd begun packing.

I filled a Waterford tumbler with ice and poured Scotch over it for Cal. Then filled another with ice and water for myself, holding it briefly against my forehead. I don't suppose it actually sizzled. It just seemed as if it had. Outside, the temperature was dropping like a stone; maybe Cal had the heating turned up. And yet the heat seemed to come from within and, desperate to cool down, I picked up a cube of ice, tipping back my head to slide it over the pulse hammering at my neck, over my throat, groaning with relief.

An echoing sound, softer—the merest catch of breath—sent me spinning round. Cal was standing in the doorway in a white bathrobe that threw the deep tan of his throat, his bare legs, into vivid contrast. His hair had been rough towelled and stood up in a tousled ruff. His eyes, hot enough to melt permafrost, didn't leave my face as he crossed wide acres of floor, his bare feet making no sound as he closed the gap between us.

CHAPTER EIGHT

You've made a total fool of yourself over the man of your dreams. Do you:
a. sigh, tell him it's his fault for being so sexy and remind him that if he ever changes his mind he's got your phone number?
b. avoid, for the rest of your life, every possible location where you might meet?
c. change your name and your hair colour?
d. emigrate?
e. next time you meet act as if nothing happened? It takes real acting skill but if you can pull it off he'll think you're a very cool lady. He might even have a few regrets of his own…

WHEN Cal was close enough to touch, he reached for the drink I'd poured for him, swallowed half of it, then set the glass down. 'I was afraid you might be cold,' he said. 'I thought I'd better come and turn on the fire.'

Too late. A fire had been smouldering inside me from the moment I'd first set eyes on him. He'd been unwittingly fanning it ever since and his kiss was all that had been needed to turn it into an inferno.

'I'm not cold,' I said, unnecessarily. The clinging

125

black dress was too tight and I tried to ease the tight, strapless bodice in an attempt to let some cool air next to my skin.

He reached out and gripped my wrist, stopping me. 'God help me, Philly, I've tried. I've really tried, but you make it very hard to be good.'

Good? What on earth was he talking about? 'I... I was h-h-hot...' I stammered. I'd never stammered in my life...

'Tell me about it,' he said, taking the ice from my hand, running it over his own face with the flat of his hand. Over his lips.

I knew how he felt. My lips were hot, too. Hot and swollen and throbbing.

'I've just risked pneumonia,' he went on relentlessly. 'Standing under a cold shower to very little effect only to find my self-sacrifice undermined by a girl who belongs to someone else taunting me with her body.'

'No! Why would I—'

'Playing games,' he said.

'No, really. I told you. I was—'

'Hot. I heard you.' I jumped as he took the ice from his lips and touched it to my temple, a gesture of such intimacy that I felt exposed and vulnerable and I closed my eyes in an effort to shut out his anger. 'How hot?' he demanded.

I was about to burst into flames. 'Cal, don't—'

I'd made him angry. I didn't know how, or why. If he'd been any other man I'd have felt nervous, afraid even.

'Here?' he persisted, letting it slide along the edge of my jaw.

'Cal…' I protested weakly, my knees buckling beneath me. I was on my feet only because he still had my wrist clamped in his strong fingers, because he was holding me up. 'Please… I'm sorry…'

Sorry that he didn't desire me in the way I wanted. My skin was too tight for my body. My nipples were trying to escape from my dress. I wanted to tear it off, to have his cold hands on my body, holding me, touching me everywhere…

'Here?' he demanded, mercilessly, stroking the ice slowly down my throat, along the line of the brief bodice, over the mounds of my breasts so that the melting ice trickled in icy runnels down a cleavage that was threatening to burst out of its confines.

'Yes!' I shouted back, at last finding my voice. 'Yes, yes, yes! Are you happy? Does it amuse you to turn me on like the Blackpool illuminations? To have me panting for you?'

'I'm not gay, Philly,' he said, his voice a harsh warning. 'But I guess you've worked that out for yourself.'

'What?' I opened my eyes. His eyes glittered back with a raw and basic desire. Not? Not gay? Not… The questions could wait; I wanted action, not talk, and I laughed. 'You can't begin to know how relieved I am to hear that,' I said.

'Philly, listen to me! I want you to understand. You thought you were safe, but you're not. Right now you're playing with fire.'

'I'm already in flames,' I told him and I reached up, put my hands around his neck and pulled him down to me. 'Burning up.' And I kissed him. Shamelessly. Without reserve. Giving it everything I'd got.

For a moment he resisted, fought the shock of raw desire that I saw flame in his eyes. Held me off so that he could see me.

'You smell so good,' he said. Then, mercifully, he pulled me close, held me as if he would absorb me into his own body. 'So sweet.' And then his mouth, cold and tasting of Scotch, came down hard on mine, taking me somewhere dark and primitive where there were no thoughts, only feelings.

I had been so sure Cal had taught me everything there was to know about kissing when he'd rescued me from the blind date that Sophie had planned.

I'd been wrong. That had just been the trailer.

This was a master-class.

The release of my zip was a blessed relief. His mouth on my breasts, pushing away the flimsy lace as he sank to his knees, his tongue slowly circling my nipples, sucking on them so I wanted to scream out loud with the pleasure of it, trailing across my stomach, promising ecstasy, was only the most temporary relief. I felt wicked and beautiful and wanted. I felt like a woman and I wanted to become one. Truly. Now. I wanted to be naked and I wanted him, ached for him inside me.

'Cal—' His name was an urgent whisper, pleading,

demanding. Demanding things I didn't know how to ask for. 'Please—'

Maybe he misunderstood the catch in my throat. Or maybe my voice just reached through the thick haze of desire that clouded his eyes, breaking the spell. But he groaned as if in pain.

'Philly…I'm sorry…'

No-o-o!

'Don't stop,' I begged. If I could have heard myself I'd have probably been shocked at such a wanton response, but my senses had been totally subsumed under the urgency of touch and taste. Nothing existed but the honeyed sweetness of Cal's mouth taking me to places I'd only ever dreamed about, the smooth, warm flesh of his neck and shoulders beneath my hands, the manifestly urgent need I'd woken in him, that he in turn had fired in my veins. 'Please…don't stop…'

But it was too late. He was already in retreat, on his feet with space between us, chill air where a moment before there had only been heat and we had been one.

'We can't do this,' he said.

'Yes…yes, we can…' That he wanted to was plainly evident even for someone of my limited experience, making this rejection all the more incomprehensible. Painful.

'*I* can't,' he said.

'I thought you'd just admitted that you could,' I said bitterly as I realised that he meant it. Then I put my hands to my mouth, shaking my head. 'Sorry, sorry, sorry…'

'Don't! Don't say that. I'm the one who should be saying that. I thought I could handle this, but I was wrong.'

I didn't want him to be sorry. I just wanted him to keep holding me. Well, he was, but only to steady me, and as soon as he was certain that I had control over my limbs, that I wasn't about to collapse in a heap on his beautifully polished floor, he relinquished even that link. I'd never felt so alone in my life as in that moment when he stepped back, putting clear space between us. Then, before he could change his mind—or I did anything to change it for him—he turned abruptly, crossed the room, picked up the whisky glass and drained it.

It seemed like a good moment to tuck myself back in my bra, haul up the dress that was bunched around my waist. Only when the zip—horribly loud in the silence—had clicked back into place did he turn to face me.

'You're alone,' he said. It sounded like a life sentence. 'Vulnerable and alone and this is wrong. You should go home. Back to Maybridge. To Don.'

'I'm never going back,' I said.

'You don't mean that, Philly.'

Didn't I? Where the words had come from I wasn't sure—only that I was speaking the truth. I'd spent my whole adult life thinking I was in love with Don and yet here I was, just one day away from him, throwing myself at another man as if the end of the world had just been proclaimed.

Something was wrong, but it wasn't Cal. It wasn't this. Something in his stance warned me that he didn't want to hear that.

'You're just angry with him for letting you come to London without him,' he said.

I would have laughed if I hadn't been afraid that I might cry instead. There was no point in being angry with Don. I'd tried that, yelling with frustration when his mother had put a spoke in our plans for the hundredth time. He'd just looked like a puppy caught with a chewed slipper—sorry, but helpless.

There was only one man in the entire world I was angry with and he was right in front of me.

'And you think this is me getting even? Is that it?' He didn't answer, which could only mean that was precisely what he thought. 'You think that's why I was going out with Sophie?' I demanded, refusing to let him get away with silence.

'You were pretty much stripped off—' from the safety of the far side of the room he gave me a swift head-to-toe glance '—and ready for action when I waylaid you on your way out tonight.'

'And you thought you'd save me from myself, did you? For Don? Well, I'd say that was really noble of you except for one thing.' I gave him the look right back, starting with his bare feet, the soft white bathrobe that a moment before had been enfolding me, brushing against my bare skin. Almost losing my nerve, as I finally met his gaze head-on, looked him full in the eye. 'When you walked in here just now you looked pretty much ready for action yourself.'

'No, damn it—'

'No, damn you, Cal.' I snatched up my bag, digging out my phone even as I headed for the front door. I was already half in my coat by the time he caught up with me, slamming his hand against the door to stop me leaving.

I didn't bother to point out that he'd just told me to go home. I just flipped open my phone and punched redial. My fingers were shaking too much to attempt anything more complicated and it wasn't as if it mattered who answered.

'What the hell are you doing?'

'Calling a taxi. Then I'm getting on with the evening I'd planned. It could be Tony's lucky night—'

'The hell with that.' And Cal twitched the phone from my hand and held it to his ear for a moment. Someone must have answered because he said, 'Sorry, wrong number.' Then he flipped it shut before handing it back to me, barely able to suppress a grin.

'You've got a nerve,' I said.

'I've also got the number of a taxi firm a lot closer than Maybridge.'

'What?'

'Your last call was for a taxi to take you to the station?'

'Don couldn't take me.' I was pretty angry then, too. 'Something more important came up...' And then, to my embarrassment, a tear slid down my face.

Before I could dash it away, Cal had brushed his thumb over my cheek.

'He must be some kind of man to have kept you for so long with so little care.'

Maybe I'd just clung like a limpet. Refusing to let go, to accept that he didn't really want me at all, but was just too kind to say so.

'What are you doing?' I demanded as Cal reached behind me.

'Helping you into your coat.' He fed my other arm into the sleeve as if I were a two-year-old rather than twenty-two, holding it together in front of me. 'That's better,' he said. 'Now I can think clearly.'

He seemed like a man with his thoughts seriously under control to me. My own were nowhere near as composed, but, clutching what was left of my dignity to my heaving bosom, I made a move to leave. He didn't release me and I said, 'Please, I should go.'

'Where?' I raised my eyebrows, hoping to convey without words that it was really none of his business. No matter how much I wanted it to be. 'Really?' he persisted.

'To bed,' I admitted, after a tussle with my conscience. 'With a cup of cocoa and a good book.' *War and Peace* might be just about long enough for me to forget this humiliation, my complete loss of self-possession, but I wasn't banking on it. 'You're welcome to join me but you have to bring your own book,' I said flippantly. Well, he wasn't going to take me up on the offer, was he? No one was.

'I thought we were going out for supper?'

'Did you? Was that before or after we had sex?'
Well, that took the smile right off his face. Actually
it wasn't so much a smile as a gentle, maybe-we-can-
start again sort of look. He was fooling himself. We
could never go back to where we'd been. Just good
friends. 'I guess if it was after,' I said cruelly, 'we'd
have had to call out for a pizza again. Thanks, but
I'll pass, this time.'

'When did you last eat?' he persisted.

'You sound just like my mother.'

'When?'

I did that big sigh thing. 'Sophie and I had a mid-
shopping snack at the sushi bar in Harvey Nicks.
Fabulous.'

'Her choice, I imagine. Very low calorie.'

'Well, I would have probably gone for scrambled
eggs on buttered toast, given the choice,' I admitted.
'But low calorie is good. At this rate my jeans will
soon do up without straining the buttonhole.'

'Your jeans are just perfect the way they are.' I
pulled a face. 'I mean it!' he said angrily and I
flinched. He tightened his grip on my coat. 'I'm sorry.
I didn't mean to shout. But you've got to be hungry.'

Oh, yes. I was suffering from the kind of misery-
induced hunger that only serious quantities of junk
food could assuage. And I still hadn't been shopping.
Well, not that kind of shopping anyway.

'Maybe I'll have another go at the cheese on toast,'
I said, a little shakily. I found being this close to him
very disturbing. I really needed to get away.

'Oh, no,' he said. 'I'm not prepared to risk that.'

'The cooker's fixed,' I protested and then, in a determined effort to change the subject, I said, 'What
happens about the bill for that?'

'It's covered by the maintenance service contract,
but I can't guarantee to jump you to the front of the
queue again.'

'I... Thank you.'

'Don't thank me. Just sit down and try to stay out
of trouble for two minutes while I get some clothes
on.' I opened my mouth to protest. 'Please.'

I closed it again. 'Please' was good, although he
wasn't letting me go until I promised to obey him.
Maybe he thought I'd make a run for it the moment
his back was turned. He could be right about that. But
then I'd have to move out, or spend the next few
months tiptoeing around to avoid him. On tenterhooks
every time I set foot outside the apartment. Using the
stairs instead of the lift. And if I went back to
Maybridge, grovelled to my manager, begging to be
allowed to stay, what would I do with all those expensive new clothes?

'Please, Philly. I need to explain—'

No-o-o! I didn't want explanations. I
wanted...well...better not think about what I wanted.
I clearly wasn't going to get it.

'All right,' I conceded, less than gracefully. 'But I
need to make some running repairs before I go out in
public,' I said. 'I don't want to scare the locals.'

He didn't laugh at my feeble attempt at humour.
Didn't bother to reassure me that I looked fine, either.

He simply reached out and opened the door to the guest cloakroom. 'Help yourself.'

Alone with my reflection, I tried to work out what it was about me that made me so...resistible.

I had all the basic equipment. None of it spectacular, admittedly. Apart from my hair, but the least said about that, the better. Eyes, two. Basic brown with the requisite lashes and brows. At least those had escaped the ginger curse. Nose, just the one and, while it wasn't an especially 'cute' version, it was neat and functional. Even the freckles were under control at this time of year. Mouth...

Actually my mouth looked different. Or maybe it just felt that way. Fuller, softer, well kissed. And a cat-like little smile that I couldn't quite control tucked up the corners as I let my mind replay the moment, remember just how thoroughly kissed it had been.

Maybe I should concentrate on that, I decided and, having dealt with smudged mascara, I reapplied the red lipstick that Sophie had picked out for me. It was something I'd never tried before. I'd always thought redheads should avoid wearing bright red. Clearly I was wrong. That, at least, had been a big success.

Cal was ready to go in his long dark overcoat when I finally emerged from the cloakroom. He just looked at me for a moment and I thought he was going to say something. Whatever it was, he bit it back; I know he did because I saw his jaw tighten before he turned abruptly away and opened the front door, standing well back to give me plenty of room to get through it without brushing against him.

'Where are we going?' I asked, when the silence had gone on too long.

'What? Oh, just a local place. I booked a table earlier this afternoon. That's why I called you, to ask you if you'd have dinner with me. Before...' He stopped, clearly unwilling to say before *what*. We both knew before *what*.

That wouldn't do. Not if it wasn't going to remain a constant minefield, something to be avoided at all costs. I'd done the quiz, checked the high-scoring answers so that I could learn by my mistakes. No tiger would let something like that fester.

'BK?' I prompted.

'What?'

'Before Kiss,' I said, with what was supposed to be amused laughter. All he had to do, according to the magazine, was laugh along with me and we could remain friends.

Maybe he didn't understand the concept, or maybe I sounded hysterical rather than amused. Or maybe it was just bad luck that the lift came to a halt at that moment and I stepped out into the lobby, carefully avoiding the crack in my new high-heeled shoes and drawing unnecessary attention to them.

I saw him staring at them and said, 'They're new. Sophie did a great job, don't you think?'

'Very pretty. But can you walk in them?'

'I'm going to be in trouble on Monday if I can't.' Then, before he could say it, 'So, nothing new there.'

'It's the male staff at Bartlett's who'll be in trouble,' he said enigmatically.

'How far is "local"?' I asked, ignoring this veiled suggestion that I was intent on laying waste the entire male population of London before retiring to domesticity and Don. I knew my limitations. They'd just been demonstrated most succinctly.

'Just round the corner.'

Which could mean anything, but I gave him the benefit of the doubt. 'Then let's go.'

I didn't wait to see if he was following me, but strode out in my apparently dangerous new shoes as if wearing four-inch-heels came to me as naturally as breathing. I'd never tried them before because Don wasn't that tall.

They felt great.

He still beat me to the door, then stood back holding it for a tall, incredibly elegant woman who was on her way in.

'Cal! Darling!' she exclaimed, kissing his cheek, holding his arms in a proprietorial manner that had all my little green cells hissing with 'hands-off' fury. Considering that I hadn't known they existed until today, they were getting quite an airing.

'Tessa,' he said. 'You're looking good.'

'So are you. In fact you look terrific. When did you get back? Why haven't you called? Do the Aged Parents know you're home? They're in London.'

'A couple of days ago. I've been busy. They wouldn't be interested,' he said, replying to her questions with a discouraging minimum of vocabulary, which appeased the green cells a little.

Ms Tall-and-Elegant did not take offence, however,

she simply shook her head slightly, as if in exasperation, then glanced at me, lifting a perfectly groomed eyebrow. 'Not that busy,' she said, with a smile that, while speculative, was not possessive and offering a perfectly manicured hand that had clearly never been near a kitchen sink.

'Tessa, this is Philly Gresham. She's moved in with the Harrington girls for a few months while her parents are away. We're going to Nico's for supper. Philly this is my sister, Tessa Cartwright. Presumably on a sortie from darkest Yorkshire to lay waste to Knightsbridge in the true spirit of Christmas.'

She gave him the kind of look that sisters reserved for brothers before saying, 'Good to meet you, Philly.' She held my hand for a moment. 'If you need anything I'm at number sixty-four. Just knock.' Then to her brother, 'If you can spare the time, you can take me out to dinner before I return to the frozen north, Cal. Catch up on family gossip.' And with a wave she headed for the lift.

I stepped through the door he was still holding, shivering a little, and not just at the sudden drop in temperature.

'Cold?'

'It was a mistake to come out without my thermals,' I said.

'Not from where I was standing.' He put his hand to my back, directing me to the left, then took my arm, tucking it beneath his, presumably for warmth. 'It's not far.'

It would have been petty to object, or pull away.

We'd walked linked together like this through Kensington Gardens, when I'd thought he could have no interest in me as a woman, and I'd felt cherished.

What had changed?

Everything, I realised. I could have dismissed the first kiss as another of his Galahad rescues. But he wasn't gay and that second kiss had been personal. He'd meant it.

And so had I.

Cal was greeted as an old friend as we entered the small and cosy restaurant a couple of minutes later. He was surrounded by people who knew him, it seemed. I'd thought I'd known him. But I didn't.

Oh, I knew that he was kind, that he was fun to be with. That he was a great kisser. They weighed pretty heavily on the plus side. But I also knew he'd deceived me, allowed me to believe he was Kate and Sophie's 'sweet' gay neighbour. Why, for heaven's sake?

He hadn't even bothered to mention that his sister had an apartment in the same block. I hadn't even known he had a sister!

I'd told him my whole damn life story. Okay, so I'd lived a pretty uneventful life and there wasn't much to tell, but I still felt short-changed.

He hung up our coats and we went through to a tiny bar where the *maître d'* brought us menus and asked if we'd like a drink. Cal stayed with Scotch. 'And a mineral water,' he added, without bothering to ask me.

'Still or sparkling, miss?'

Something inside me snapped. 'Well, gosh,' I said, laying my hand against my breast, quite deliberately drawing attention to the low cut of the dress, my bare arms and naked shoulders. 'Do you think the excitement of *sparkling* water might just be too much for me?' I wasn't plagued with the kind of temper that traditionally went with red hair, but I was beginning to feel as if someone had lit a short fuse beneath me. I know I'd *said* I was on water for the duration, but I was a woman. Changing my mind went with the chromosomes.

'I'm sorry, Philly, I assumed you meant it when you said you were sticking to water. What would you like?' Cal's coolness in the face of my bad behaviour, and doubtless intended to defuse it, had the opposite effect.

'A cocktail. A Woo Woo,' I added casually, as if cocktails were something I drank on a regular basis. The only reason I'd even heard of it was because my sister—a natural-born tiger if ever there was one—had made a jugful for her hen-night. I wasn't even sure what it contained beyond Peach Schnapps and possibly Vodka, but it sounded appropriately off-the-wall and my recollection, which was admittedly rather dim—it had been one heck of a party—was that it looked pretty and tasted even better.

The man was good—I'd have missed the merest flicker of a glance in Cal's direction for confirmation if I hadn't been looking for it—before he said, 'A Woo Woo. Yes, miss.'

The drinks arrived with commendable swiftness,

along with tiny appetisers. Cal made no comment as I sipped mine, nibbled on a salted almond, merely enquiring blandly what I'd like to eat. I told him. He ordered food, deliberated over the choice of wine. By the time we'd finished our drinks the table was ready and we were shown to a secluded corner of the restaurant. Maybe the *maître d'* was worried that I'd start throwing the china.

'I bought you something today,' Cal said, when we were settled with our first course and the waiter had departed.

'Oh?' I concentrated on my salmon mousse while he took a small package from his pocket and placed it on the table between us.

It had been elaborately gift-wrapped, with an extravagant knot of curled silver ribbons.

Damn! I'd just wound myself up to be really, really mad at him and he had to choose that moment to demonstrate that he'd been thinking about me. As if I needed any more proof. I had messages backed up on my mobile showing me how much he'd been thinking. He'd even booked a table for dinner...

'Very pretty,' I said wryly. 'I'd have asked if you did the bow yourself, but clearly you didn't.'

'Okay, I deserved that...I'm sorry.'

'That's it? You're *sorry*? Have you any idea of the embarrassment I felt when I thought I'd let slip that stupid nickname—?'

He reached out, caught my hand briefly to stop me. 'I know,' he said.

'I wanted to curl up and die—'

'I know,' he repeated, still in that same reasonable voice.

'I have no doubt you thought it was hilarious.'

'If you could have seen your face…' He let it go. 'I guess you had to be there,' he said.

'I was.'

'Look, the pizza was getting cold and I didn't want to spend the rest of the evening in the hall. I promise you I had intended to put you out of your misery the minute I'd opened the wine. After that…well…I was going to offer to show you around. Ask you to have dinner with me. Or go to the theatre maybe…'

'Embark on a flirtation? Something to pass the time until you depart for the South Seas to film the life and death of the leatherback turtle.'

'Something like that,' he replied steadily, but my stupid heart still gave a leap at the thought of what 'something' might entail. However briefly. 'And then you started talking about your boyfriend.'

'Those damned anchovies,' I said, wishing I'd kept my mouth shut. Except of course I'd subconsciously been making the point that I might be stupid, but I wasn't a total loss as a woman. Overkill. Apparently he'd already noticed.

My mistake.

'From the way you talked about him, it was clear that you've been with him for years, that you're committed to a life with him. Only a complete heel would have made a play for you when you were on your own and vulnerable.'

'Oh, I see.' He was being noble. How rare. How unlikely. 'So what happened tonight?' I said.

CHAPTER NINE

You have to tell the man in your life that you're dumping him for someone new. Do you:
a.   look him in the eye, tell him what's happened, that you're sorry to hurt him in this way because he's a great bloke, but you just don't love him any more?
b.   ask his best friend to break the news to him?
c.   let him catch you in the arms of your new amour...but only if you're sure he won't turn violent?
d.   stop answering his calls and hope he'll eventually get the message?
e.   send him a 'Dear John' letter and then go and visit your granny while he gets over it?

IT WAS like poking a sore tooth. Whatever he'd been going to do, Cal had clearly had second thoughts. And third ones. But he had, if only momentarily, forgotten all his good intentions and kissed me. Done rather more than kiss me. My body was still singing from his touch.

'I'm not made of wood, Philly. Have you any idea what you looked like with your head tilted back, your hair loose over your bare shoulders, running that piece of ice over your throat?'

The picture he painted was shocking, nothing like the Philly Gresham who'd left home on Friday afternoon, fed up and angry. 'I wasn't performing for an audience,' I said, trying to justify myself. 'And when you kiss a girl, even when you're pretending, well…' I lifted my shoulders, then grabbed the front of my dress as it nearly lost its precarious battle with gravity under the strain. 'I was hot,' I said.

I'd invited him to tell me he hadn't been pretending. He didn't. What he said was, 'It won't happen again.'

It wasn't what I wanted to hear.

'The pretend kiss? Or the one that wasn't?' I was living dangerously, I knew it, but I couldn't help myself. I wanted him to want me. I wanted him to want me so much that nothing, short of the end of the world, would deter him from making love to me.

'Both. What you needed last night, above all else, was a friend, Philly,' he said carefully, and avoiding my question. 'I wanted you to be able to relax with me. Feel safe. Not to have to keep up your guard against a man with more than pizza on his mind.'

I did. I do, I thought. Feel safe. But knowing that wasn't doing anything to cool me down. Knowing that he was caring and thoughtful as well as hot and sexy made the prospect of surrender irresistible.

He was a dangerous man, no doubt. I felt alive when I was with him, aroused and weak with longing for him to do things to me that should have made me blush with shame. But deep down, where it really mattered, I felt totally safe. Protected, cared for. He'd already demonstrated that he would put my best interests before his own gratification. And mine. And I knew that if he loved me I would be the most fortunate woman in the world. I also knew, instinctively, that he wasn't the kind of man to settle down in Maybridge. Fulfil my dream of small-town domesticity. But then that was the dream of the mouse who'd left home on Friday.

I'd been kissed by Callum McBride and I wasn't the same girl any more.

'I realised,' he went on, although he seemed to be struggling a bit as I fanned myself with my hand, 'that if I left you with the impression that I was gay, you wouldn't think of me as a threat.'

He waited for me to confirm that he'd got it right.

I was going to repeat the careless shrug, but recollected myself in time and said, 'You did a fine job.' We'd flirted and laughed and he'd put his arm around me but I'd thought, hey, this is okay. I'm safe as houses. I'm not doing anything bad. But I hadn't wanted to be. Safe.

'I also realised,' he said, 'that if you felt safe, I could stay close to you.'

'Really?' I went for a thoughtful frown with that 'really' to prevent a wide grin from breaking out all over my face. As if I was interested in his thought processes rather than over the moon that he liked me enough to make such a sacrifice to spend time with me.

A man who could do that had to be very confident of his masculinity. Had to be able to laugh at himself.

I thought how easy it would be to love a man like that.

'Really,' he said. 'And it wasn't noble at all, Philly. I wanted to stay close. I wanted to touch you, put my arm around you. I wanted to see you laugh. Wanted you to tell me the kind of secrets you'd only tell a friend.'

'You don't think straight men and women can be just good friends?' I said, before he could get onto secrets.

His smile was wry. 'I think we've already proved how impossible it is. I kept up the charade for twenty-four hours before I completely lost it. And even then you weren't fooled, just confused.'

I was a lot more than that, but I let it go. 'Sure I was confused. You were flirting with me this morning over breakfast,' I said, thinking of the way he'd played with my hair. Held onto my hand. Flattered me, even. 'Was that unintentional? Were you aware that you were doing it?'

'I…I guess I just couldn't help it,' he said. 'Any more than you could help the look you gave that girl in the market.'

'You saw that?' I demanded. Then wished I hadn't as my cheeks flooded with colour.

'If you'd been convinced I was gay, you wouldn't have bothered. You'd have been amused, or a little sad for her. You wouldn't have been sending hands-off signals. Is that why you didn't answer my messages, Philly?' I frowned. 'Were you feeling guilty about Don?'

'I didn't go straight back to the flat,' I said obliquely, not ready to admit that the only man in my thoughts had been him. 'I went to the Science Museum.'

'Oh,' he said. 'I see.' As if I'd just unlocked the secret to my deepest thought processes. Completely betrayed myself. Maybe I had.

'They've got a baby Austin on show there. Like the one Don's restoring. He asked me to go and have a look at it. Send him a picture postcard.'

'I'm sorry.'

'That I sent him a postcard?'

'That you felt guilty.'

'Why? It's not your fault.' He had nothing to reproach himself for. Well, maybe he had, but any guilty feelings I might have had weren't his responsibility. They were one hundred per cent my own. 'And to be honest I don't know what I felt.' Okay, so I was stretching the truth a little, but in a good cause. 'Confused, mostly.'

'Everything all right, sir?' The young waiter whisked away our plates, having ascertained that we'd finished. Neither of us had exactly wiped our plates clean.

'Fine,' Cal said. 'Thank you.' There was a lull while the second course was served, our glasses were filled. I regarded the wine with suspicion. Cal saw my look and said, 'It's white.'

'Lovely.' Having insisted on a cocktail, I could hardly remind him that I was sticking to water. But I'd have to be careful. This conversation was going a lot faster than anything I was used to. And I had no experience of dissembling, playing games, sexual teasing. I was conscious of laying myself bare. Exposing myself to the intensity of Cal's gaze in a way that was far more complex, more revealing than the mere unzipping of a dress. 'Can I open this now?' I asked, taking advantage of the break in conversation to pick up the gift he'd bought me.

He looked as if he wanted to say more, but he let it go. 'It's yours,' he said. 'Do what you like with it.'

I tore off the paper, but kept the ribbon safe. I already knew that I'd keep that bow, tucked away somewhere, for the rest of my life. Inside the wrapping was a small flat box that contained a keyring. Hanging from the keyring was a miniature, state-of-the-art attack alarm.

Not a fun thing like the one my mother had bought, but a serious piece of kit made from the kind of dull black metal that no shoe, even a Callum-McBride-sized shoe, could dent, let alone destroy.

'It's to replace the one I flattened with my size elevens,' he said, his thoughts evidently running along the same lines as my own.

'Elevens?' I lifted my eyebrows. I was getting this whole tiger thing down to a fine art, but it was more than that. I knew I mustn't let him see how much his gesture meant to me. Or he'd be the one racked with the guilt. 'I'd have said…bigger.'

And even in that softly lit, discreet little restaurant I could have sworn that his cheekbones were stained with a darker red. It made me feel powerful and strong and suddenly very much in control.

'Do you think I'm safe with this in an enclosed space?' I asked as I laid the little keyring beside my plate, my thumb brushing gently over the alarm.

'If you feel threatened, just press the button.'

I laughed. 'You like to live dangerously, don't you?'

'It beats the alternative.'

'How would you know?' I asked. 'You've been living dangerously ever since you used one of your mother's best sheets to make a hide and escape your architectural destiny.'

'Unlike you with your safe job, safe boyfriend, safe life?' He shook his head. 'Forget I said that. If that's what you want, who am I to criticise?'

Did I? Want it?

'I've left home, got a terrifying new job, and a pile of smart new clothes to go with it, thank you very much.' Okay, so the boyfriend needed work, but I thought I was doing pretty well for a little over twenty-four hours into a new life.

'You're in a flat your mother found for you and you were, by your own admission, seconded to Bartlett's kicking and screaming. I hate to break it to you, darling, but it takes more than one ruined sheet to escape your destiny.'

'That's out of the Cal McBride book of homespun philosophy, is it? Very profound.'

'I'm merely making the point that it's easier to stay

with what you have, what you know, than take a leap into the dark.'

'You didn't. Take the safe option.'

'I came close,' he admitted. 'I sold my soul for my cameras, the light meters, lenses, tripod that I begged as birthday and Christmas presents. Sold it with assurances that it was just a hobby. It wouldn't affect my school work. Easy promises that I'd go to university, qualify as an architect. Join the family firm.'

'Did you mean to keep them?'

'Architecture, especially as the partner of a major firm, is a lot more lucrative than filming pigeons. I knew that. I thought I could live with it, be content making small films in my spare time. I thought I could have it all and for two years I applied myself to becoming the son my parents wanted me to be.'

'What changed?'

'Someone I met at university...' he looked at me then, as if weighing his words, as if it was important that I understood '...someone clever, lovely, talented, was killed in a stupid accident. She slipped on icy steps and broke her neck racing to get to a lecture she didn't even want to go to. One minute she was full of life, warmth. The next she was dead.'

'I'm so sorry, Cal—' I wanted to reach out for him, comfort him, but I felt it would have been intrusive. That I didn't know him well enough for that.

'She was twenty-one—not even your age, Philly— and studying mathematics instead of music to please her father. He'd insisted she shouldn't waste her fine brain on something as pointless as singing.' He shook his head. 'She had a voice that could make you want to laugh, or weep. The world is full of mathematicians…'

'You loved her.'

He stirred. 'Perhaps. In that careless way of the young who believe themselves to be immortal. My grief, I suspect, was as much for the loss of that innocence as for her death.'

He shrugged, but I thought he was playing down his own hurt.

'All I know is that she wasted her gift to fit someone else's vision of her life and as I stood by her graveside I made her a promise that I wouldn't do the same.'

And he reached out and took my hand then, as if he needed me to understand, and I turned it in his, grasping his fingers in mine so that he would know that I did. And, intuitively, I realised something else.

'That's it, isn't it?' I said. 'Your deep secret. The one thing you've never told anyone else?'

'Smart, aren't you?'

'As paint,' I assured him. Then, because I wasn't ready to tell him mine, because frankly I didn't think he'd believe me if I did, especially not after this evening, I said, 'So what happened?'

'I left university.'

'And no one said a word? You suggested that your mother wasn't exactly overwhelmed by your career choice and when your sister asked you if you'd seen your family…' I left it there.

'Okay. There was a major row. My mother sug-

gested I take a year out. Give myself time to get it
out of my system. She thought a year as an assistant
cameraman on a film crew, out in all weathers, working for someone else instead of pleasing myself,
would be enough to dampen my enthusiasm. My father knew better. He knew that if I left university, I'd
never go back.'

'He tried to hold you to your promise?'

'He was cleverer than that. He offered me my flat
as a gift, just to complete my degree. He asked nothing more than that. Just take my degree, then we'd
talk again.'

'Your flat? You mean number seventy-two?'

'He designed the apartment complex.'

'It's beautiful, Cal.'

'He won an award for it. We McBrides are high
achievers.' He grinned. 'Of course, being talented
helps, and he's not just talented, he's clever. The de-
veloper got into trouble and Dad bailed him out in
return for a share of the real estate. They use the
penthouse when they're in London. Tessa was given
the smaller flat on the floor below us as a wedding
present. She and her husband use it as a *pied-à-terre*
when they come down from his estate in Yorkshire.
And I was offered number seventy-two in return for
giving up all this airy-fairy filming nonsense.'

Now I was confused. 'But if you turned him
down—'

'I bought it myself when it came on the market a
couple of years ago. A declaration that I'd made it in
my own way, on my own two feet.'

I sucked air through my teeth.

'Bad move, you think?'

'Well, you tell me. Did your father knock on your door, shake your hand and say "Well done, son…"?'

He acknowledged my understanding with the slightest movement of his head. 'If he did, I must have been out. Clever, talented and stubborn as hell.'

'And you don't take after him, I suppose?'

'What, me?' His laughter, I thought, seemed a little forced.

'Don't let it fester, Cal.'

'I've tried—'

'No, you haven't. You've waved your success in his face like a red flag at a bull. You've effectively said "See? Here I am and I did it all by myself. I don't need you." A little humility would go a long way, don't you think? Some acknowledgement that you're the man you are because that's how he made you. Clever, talented and stubborn as hell.'

'Please, don't mince your words, Philly. If you think I made a mistake, just say so.'

'You don't need me to tell you what you've done. Just imagine standing by his graveside ten, twenty years from now,' I said, taking him back to his own moment of truth. 'Imagine how you'd feel, knowing you could have healed the breach but chose to wrap yourself in pride. That should do it.' He flinched and I squeezed his hand to let him know I understood that it wasn't easy. 'It'll be Christmas soon,' I said. 'It's a time for big gestures.'

'What are you suggesting? That I have myself gift-wrapped and delivered?'

I thought I'd said more than enough. Blamed the Woo Woo and a glass of wine. 'I'd say if you've got any ideas along those lines, you should have yourself delivered to me. Unfortunately I'll be sharing a turkey drumstick with my Great-Aunt Alice this year and I doubt her heart would stand the excitement.'

My own would be put to the test.

Then, because I was in grave danger of dying of embarrassment all over again, because I had to say something to fill the apparently endless silence that followed this stupid remark, I retrieved my fingers on the pretext of tucking away a stray curl and said, 'Lecture over. So, tell me, Cal, who, exactly, is Gorgeous George? And if Jay isn't your "partner"…' and I did those quote marks with my fingers '…why did he do his best to kill me with a single look?'

And, having thoroughly changed the subject, I picked up my fork, making a determined assault on my supper and, after a moment, Cal followed suit.

'I leased the flat to George Mathieson while I was in Africa,' he said. 'He moved out last week. I imagine he's your man.'

'Well,' I persisted, 'he's George. But is he gorgeous?'

'He was a terrific tenant.' I just looked at him. 'Okay, he's an actor-stroke-male-model, six foot two, with eyes so blue that contact lenses had to have been involved and cheekbones you could chisel marble with.'

'A simple "yes" would have done.'

He grinned. 'You don't have to worry, Philly. He's really not my type.'

'No?' I resisted the urge to ask him to describe his "type" and laughed obediently. 'And Jay?'

'I really couldn't speak for Jay. Maybe you should ask his wife.'

'Wife? You mean he's *married*?'

'You seem surprised.'

He was teasing. I was catching on fast. 'So,' I said, 'if he wasn't jealous, what was his problem this morning?'

'He wanted me to come and take a look at his first cut of the film. I told him I had a previous commitment. One I wasn't prepared to break.'

'It had nothing to do with the umbrella?'

'He never even mentioned it,' Cal admitted. 'I gave him the one you bought this morning and he didn't notice the difference.'

'But why was he so...' I dredged my brain for a word that would cover his attitude towards me '...tetchy? If he wasn't being possessive he was being downright rude.'

'It wasn't personal, Philly. He's obsessive about his work. He'd been working half the night and he was seriously irritated that I put you before the opportunity to tell him how brilliant he is.'

I allowed myself a momentary mental whoop at that, then said, 'I'm sorry, but I don't get it. Why did you go to all that bother choosing a replacement this morning?'

'Well, I had to buy him a new one. The longer I took over choosing it, the longer I could enjoy your company. Putting you in that taxi and letting you go was the hardest thing I've done in a long time.'

I forced myself to concentrate on eating in order to keep the whoops under control.

'Jay distracted me for a moment after your taxi pulled away, banging on his window, furious because I was late, and when I turned back you and your taxi had disappeared. It was as if you'd stepped out of my life and for a moment my heart just stopped—'

He came abruptly to a halt as if aware he'd betrayed more of his feelings than he'd intended, but the warm glow that spread through me made the restaurant's heating redundant. I could have walked along the riverside frontage of the apartment without my coat, just as long as Cal was there with his arm in mine.

'It was stupid, I know, but when you didn't answer my messages I began to imagine every conceivable catastrophe. In the end I cut short the editing session—'

'Oh, thanks. Now Jay really will hate me.'

'No. He's obsessive, not inhuman. He could see my mind was somewhere else. He told me to go away and sort my life out while he got on with the important stuff.' I suddenly felt very warm towards the man. 'I just wanted to see you, reassure myself that you were safe.'

'I'm not a complete idiot, Cal. I can get from point

A to point B without someone to hold my hand.' It was more fun that way, though.

He lifted his hands in a gesture that looked very much like surrender. 'I guess I'm the idiot. The truth is I just wanted to see you. Look at you, even though I knew I mustn't touch.'

I hadn't been aware of any reluctance to touch. Or maybe I was just suddenly conscious of how rarely Don touched me. Just reached out to touch my hand, or my face, or my hair...

'Then the lift doors opened and I saw you looking like something out of my wildest dreams, but not for me, not even for your terminally careless boy next door, but just for a night out clubbing with Sophie Harrington and her friends, and I lost my head. That's why I kissed you. If you were available I wanted you for myself.'

'You could have had me, Cal,' I pointed out gently.

'And afterwards? You felt guilty about a little flirting. If I'd taken advantage of your...'

'What?'

'I was going to say innocence.' He let the word hang between us for a moment and I thought he'd guessed my secret and I held my breath, afraid that the wrong word or movement would betray me. Then he shook his head. 'I guess I mean vulnerability.' Then he lifted his shoulders as if that wasn't quite right either. 'You'd have hated me for that, Philly. But nowhere near as much as I'd have hated myself.'

'You asked me why I didn't return your messages.' He'd just bared his soul and I could do no less, but it was hard, like stripping myself naked in public. 'You put me in that cab, then you kissed my cheek.' I touched the place, still feeling the slight roughness of his chin against my skin. The mingled scent of soap and leather and fresh air. 'I thought for a moment you were going to stay. That you were going to say to hell with Jay, get in the cab beside me and take things a whole lot further. It was madness, I knew it was madness, but I wanted you so much that it was an ache.'

'I wanted to—'

'But you didn't. You stepped back and turned away even before the cab pulled away from the kerb. And when I turned to look back out of the cab window you were looking up at Jay, hand raised to him, and I felt as if you'd forgotten I existed the minute you shut the door.'

'No!'

'I felt so…jealous. I knew I had no right to feel that way, but I couldn't help it.'

I'd been twisting a strand of hair round and round my finger and he caught my hand, stopped me, unravelled the curl. Kept my hand in his.

'So I went to the Science Museum and sat there for a while, looking at the baby Austin and remembered all the evenings, weekends, I'd spent in a cold garage watching Don working on his restoration project. All the evenings and weekends through the years as he'd played with broken-down machines, bringing them back to life.'

'Why did you do it?' I looked up. 'Not the museum. The years.'

'Because at ten years old I hero-worshipped him. Because at thirteen I was infatuated with this blond giant. Because he never told me to go away and stop bothering him the way my brothers did. Never tormented me with spiders. Was always kind. Because we were friends. Best friends. Because…'

I looked into the void. It was a dark and dangerous place with no guarantees. And I stepped into it.

'Because having declared to the entire world at the age of ten that I was going to marry him, it never occurred to me that I wouldn't.'

'He should never have let you out of his sight.'

I was beginning to wonder if he'd notice that I'd gone. He might miss the flasks of hot coffee I made for him, the fact that he didn't have to make any effort to get a life. All he had to do was tag along with me and it happened. And sometimes even that had seemed like an effort when some flange sprocket had needed his attention.

I'd been spared the tempestuous tears of my sister's, my friends', heartbreak dramas, smugly avoiding the relationship lows, safe in my own little make-believe world. But I was only just beginning to discover how much I'd missed out on the highs, too.

It had taken just one kiss from Cal McBride to show me exactly what I'd been missing.

Not that I was fooling myself. I'd thrust myself into his life and I was different enough to catch his attention, but he was a rolling stone, not the home-maker

I'd set my heart on. He'd be leaving in a few weeks, or months.

Whether the new woman, the tiger he'd woken inside me, had brought to life with a kiss, was strong enough to deal with that, I didn't know. But I'd lived in the safe little cocoon of my own making for long enough. How closely wrapped I hadn't realised. I'd take the risk…

'Philly?'

'What?' I realised I'd been wool-gathering. 'Sorry, I was miles away. Did you say something?'

'In Maybridge?' he enquired, ignoring my question. Then, 'With Don,' he added, heavily. He had every right to be vexed, I thought. He was giving me his undivided attention and my mind was all over the place.

'No…' I realised I hadn't sounded exactly convincing. 'Yes, I suppose so. I have to go home, Cal.'

'Home?' I nodded. 'That's it?' he said. 'Decision made?'

'Decision made,' I said. 'I have to. We've been…' I sought a word that would explain what we'd been. 'Together' and 'partners' had a new meaning these days, taken over by people living together to replace the 'married' word. 'We've been friends for a long time. I can't just—'

'Please…you don't have to justify yourself to me.' He glanced at my plate. 'Finished?' he asked.

'I didn't mean I wanted to go this minute,' I said.

'I know what you meant, Philly,' he said. His jaw

tightened momentarily. Then, politely, 'Do you want a pudding? Coffee?'

I'd been looking forward to something rich with chocolate, but it was obvious he wanted to leave and I shook my head.

'Then let's go.'

The next few minutes were covered by the flurry of credit cards and coats. Of Nico himself appearing to assure himself that the food had been satisfactory, that nothing was wrong.

Cal, after that momentary flash of irritation, was charm personified. Taking the blame on himself for being too tired to enjoy his supper. Easing me into my coat, taking my arm as we crossed the road and leaving it there as we walked round the corner to the elegant building his father had designed, and where we now lived next door to each other.

Nothing outwardly had changed and yet I sensed that I'd said something, done something to bring the evening to a premature close.

Everything had been fine until I'd said I had to go home. But surely he could see that I couldn't just write Don a 'Dear John' letter? That I had to see him. Look him in the eye when I told him that, whatever happened in my future, he wasn't going to be part of it.

CHAPTER TEN

You've been swept off your feet by a man you've only just met. It's dangerous and exciting and your friends have warned that it's all going to end in tears—your tears. Do you:

a. throw caution to the wind? You only live once and one swift, bright rocket to the stars that you'll remember all your life is worth a thousand low energy light bulbs.

b. accept that men and tears come as a twin-pack? At least this time they'll be worth it.

c. just laugh? The guy is going to wine you and dine you and make you feel like a million dollars. What's to cry about?

d. cry, because you know it's true?

e. tell them that to risk your heart, offer it freely, selflessly, is what makes us human? And if we're hurt in the process, well, that's human, too.

CAL stopped outside my door. 'When will you go?'

'The sooner the better. Tomorrow, I guess.'

'The trains are hell on Sundays.'

They'd suit the day, then. 'I'll cope.'

'You don't have to. If you've made up your mind to go…' He paused, took a breath, as if it was an effort, but as I reached out to touch his arm, concerned, he raised it to rake his hand distractedly through his hair. 'If you're quite sure, then I'll drive you,' he said. 'Eleven? Will that give you time to get yourself together?'

Time? Did he think I was going to dress up for the occasion? Make a real effort with my hair, the full make-up job, just to show Don what he was losing?

'Thanks, but don't you think that would be a little insensitive?' Turning up on the doorstep to dump him with the new man in my life in tow.

'You might just spare a little of that sensitivity for my feelings.' I must have looked confused because he said, 'I wouldn't have a minute's peace worrying about you.'

'No?'

'No,' he said.

'Oh, right.' I was touched, but, really, this whole thing about me being totally unable to cross the road without help was getting out of hand. 'I can't imagine how I survived nearly twenty-three years without you to supervise my transport arrangements. Not even my mother worries about me the way you do.'

'Believe me, my feelings are not in the least bit motherly.' And his eyes flared momentarily with a heat that took my own breath away. 'I just can't bear the thought of you sitting in a cold, draughty train. Being diverted and delayed by track maintenance work. Think of me as a taxi service if that'll help.'

'No, Cal. Really. This is something I have to do on my own.' Then, because he looked so frustrated at my refusal to be coddled, 'You can take me to the station, if you like.' He agreed to this so readily that I knew he'd insist on coming all the way with me. Waiting for me in the station buffet so that we could repeat the journey in reverse. Together. I wanted to hug him, but he was keeping his distance. 'Just to the station, Cal,' I insisted. Then, 'Please tell me that you understand why I can't...' I stopped. 'Well, why I have to do this.'

'You want me to lie to you? I won't do that.'

'Try,' I said. Not to lie—of course I didn't want him to lie—but to see why, in the cooler light of reason, I had to close one relationship before I could embark on another. Maybe he was just mad he hadn't taken the opportunity when it had presented itself. When I'd been hot and reason had gone into melt-down.

I realised he was holding out his hand for my key, and I opened my bag, fumbling through the jumble of make-up, purse, phone to find it.

'Sorry, it's here somewhere...' I put my phone into his waiting hand. And my new scarlet lipstick. 'I don't—' About to say understand, I thought better of it and turned to my coat pocket with an apologetic look. It contained only the alarm he'd given me. 'I know I picked it up.' I went through the bag again while he waited patiently and tried not to think about how many times I'd tried that patience in the last twenty-four hours. When he'd offered me his taxi. When I'd let go of Jay's umbrella and it had been whisked away by a gust of wind. When I'd opened my door and screamed with fright… 'I didn't want to rely on Sophie,' I said, in an attempt to reassure him that I wasn't just being ditzy. 'I made sure I had it.'

'Maybe you dropped it in my place. When you pulled out your phone,' he said, reminding me of my dramatic exit bid. 'Or in the cloakroom?'

'I suppose it's possible.'

He handed back the contents of my bag and then walked towards his own front door where he produced his key from his own pocket as if to demonstrate how simple it was. I followed more slowly, still searching through my bag, rechecking the zipped compartments methodically, one by one as he opened his door.

'It's not here,' he said, stepping inside, glancing down at the richly patterned rug in the hall. 'Do you want to look in the cloakroom?'

I checked the surface around the sunken basin. Checked the floor. Checked the basket where I'd thrown the tissue on which I'd blotted my lipstick. Checked behind the door.

Nothing.

Cal lifted his brows as I emerged. 'Any luck?' I just shook my head. 'I'll call Nico's. You might have dropped it there.'

'I never opened my bag in Nico's.' I looked around my feet at the strongly patterned tribal rug that filled his wide hall. 'You're sure it's not here?' It would be easy enough to miss in the pattern.'

'Check for yourself if you want,' he said, shrugging out of his coat. As he reached up to hook it over the peg I was, for a moment, caught in a surreal moment of *déjà vu*. I'd been here before. He'd turn, begin to unbutton his cuffs, tug his shirt out of his trousers… I began to feel that same heat stealing through my limbs, curling through my body. 'I'm going to make some coffee,' he said, jerking me back to reality.

'Right,' I said.

And I kicked off my shoes, got down on my knees, stroking shaky hands across the silky pile of the rug. He was right, the key wasn't there. I was beginning to think that I must have confused the thought with the act of putting it into my bag.

Maybe he was right. Maybe I wasn't fit to leave the house on my own. Maybe I was going mad.

I joined Cal in the kitchen, hunched myself on a stool at the breakfast bar, my coat pulled tight around me, watching him make coffee.

'Sophie won't be home for hours and Kate is staying with her boyfriend,' I said.

'It's not a problem, Philly,' he said, not turning around. My heart lifted a beat. For a moment I forgot how to breathe. Telling myself that I could wait another day was one thing…being here, alone with Cal, was quite another. 'I'll make up the spare room.'

I couldn't quite bring myself to say thank you. He was being unbelievably considerate. If he was feeling even half of what I was feeling, he was being a saint. Again.

'My life used to be dull,' I said, after a while.

'I find that hard to believe.'

'It's true. I was Miss Sensible. Voted the girl most

likely to stay married to the same man all her life by
my college mates.' He looked up and met my reflection in the dark window. 'I don't think they meant it
as a compliment.'

'Not intentionally, perhaps. It seems to have been
a perceptive comment on your character.'

'Yes. They were saying I was boring. I had one
job, one boyfriend. I never drank too much, not count-
ing my sister's hen-night, which was a one-off, and I
never, ever did anything stupid like losing my front-
door key.' Then, 'Of course, it wouldn't have mattered if I had. My mother kept one with the next-door
neighbour just in case.'

'Where else?' he said. And gave his attention to
spooning coffee into a cafetière.

'Oh, not with Don's mother. They aren't exactly
chummy. Polite, yes. In a ''Good morning, Mrs
Cooper. Nice weather,'' kind of way.' My mother had
about as much time for Mrs Cooper as Mrs Cooper
had for me.

He turned to look at me, his eyes glittering, burning
with heat. Or cold. There had been a chill in his manner—nothing that an onlooker would notice, only
someone who'd felt the warmth—ever since I'd said
I had to go home.

'And?' he said, his voice as crisp and diamond
bright as the frosty air outside on his terrace.

I shivered. 'And what?'

'You were explaining how you were this paragon
who never put a foot wrong. I assumed there must be
a point.'

For a moment I considered retreat. Backing down. And then something flared in his eyes and I knew that it was heat, not cold, that was making him keep his distance. That keeping his distance was the only way he could handle this.

'And then,' I said, 'I met you.'

'You expect me to apologise for upsetting the quiet tenor of your life?'

I didn't know what I was expecting, but an apology certainly wasn't it. 'I just feel so…out of control.'

'Passion does that.'

'Passion?'

'Desire, arousal, yearning. You seemed to have the hang of it earlier this evening.' The edge to his voice softened a little.

'I did?' I asked, brightening considerably. Then I realised that Cal was regarding me with a thoughtful expression. 'Oh, I *did*,' I said, hurriedly.

'Have you talked to your mother?' he asked. 'Since you came to London?'

My mother? How had she got into this conversation? 'She called to let me know they'd arrived safely. When I was out with you this morning.'

'It's about breakfast time now in Australia,' he said. 'Why don't you ring her back?' He waved in the direction of the phone.

The temptation to call, pour out my heart, was strong, but I wasn't about to break into her grandmothering idyll with my uncertainties. 'You think she'll know what I've done with my key?' I asked.

'I think…I feel that you should talk to someone

you trust. Someone you know has only your best interests at heart. You're off balance. Don't know
where you are.' I looked around, making the point
that I knew very well where I was. 'Tell her you're
locked out and you're going to be spending the night
with a man who has designs on your virtue. Ask her
for some motherly advice.' I looked for any trace of
a smile. There didn't seem to be one. His expression
was perfectly bland, giving no clue to his thoughts.

'Have you? Designs on my virtue? You seem to
have your carnal desires under pretty tight control
from where I'm sitting.'

'Yes, well, I may be old-fashioned, but I require
your full and wholehearted co-operation,' he said, and
it seemed that, almost despite himself, a crease appeared at the corner of his mouth, precursor to a
smile. 'You've made your decision, your virtue is not
at threat. So unless you're suddenly feeling the cold,
it's quite safe to take your coat off.'

I looked down at my hands screwing the black
cashmere into a dishrag and I took it off, laid it on
the stool beside me. 'I'm so—'

'Don't!' he warned, cutting me off. 'Don't say it.
I don't want you to be sorry. About anything.'

I flinched, pulling my lips hard back between my
teeth to stop myself from saying that I was sorry, but
that I hadn't been going to say I was sorry, just confused. With an exclamation of dismay, he was at my
side, his arms around me, holding me close.

'Don't,' he whispered into my hair. 'Please don't.

I wouldn't do anything to hurt you. I want you to know that. To believe that.'

I looked up at him, then reached up and took his face between my hands. 'How could I ever doubt you, Cal?' He closed his eyes as if in pain. 'You've been my guardian angel from the moment I arrived in London. Do you think I don't know how hard it was for you to stop, take a step back when we were on the brink of making love this evening?'

'I suspect not,' he said, but scarcely above a breath. 'You can't possibly—'

'I know, Cal. I was there. I wanted you so much. Yearned for you, desired you…'

'Stop!' He pulled back, put his fingers against my lips. 'Don't say any more. Please.' And when he was sure I wouldn't say another word, he lifted his fingers from my mouth, took my hands from his face and kissed each one in turn before, quite deliberately, letting go. Then, with a wry, self-mocking little smile, 'Maybe you were right about the coat, after all. Come on, I'll find you something to wear, show you the guest room.'

Sleep was elusive. The room was lovely, the bed comfortable, but I was wrapped in a soft T-shirt that belonged to Cal McBride and his scent seemed to cling to it, enveloping me so that I was aroused, yearned, desired with every fibre, every cell, every last atom of my being.

I heard him turning restlessly in the still of the night and I hated the wall that divided us. I didn't know how I stopped myself from just going in there, climbing in beside him so that I could hold him, feel his skin, smooth and warm against me. Close and tender. An intimate discovery of how it should be between a man and woman who loved each other.

Only the belief that I was right to wait kept me pinned to my lonely bed. And the knowledge that, no matter how hard it was for both of us, Cal knew it too. He'd pulled back from the brink, made that decision for me even before I'd known I wanted to make it.

Tomorrow… I'd waited this long. I could wait another day so that we could be together without a shadow between us.

But the night seemed endless and it was light before I finally dropped off.

'Philly?' Not even the sound of a cup being placed on the bedside table was sufficient temptation to make me open my eyes. I just groaned discouragingly. 'Come on, my sweet.' Cal sat on the edge of the bed, stroking my hair in a gentle wake-up call. 'I left you as long as I could.'

My sweet? Even feeling like death, I heard the tenderness in his voice and I turned over, blinking against the light as I emerged from beneath the cocoon of the bedclothes, pushing the hair back from my face as I sat up.

'Hi,' I said, suddenly and unexpectedly shy. Expecting him to kiss me. Wanting him to kiss me.

'Hi, yourself,' he said, keeping his kisses to himself. Not taking any risks. 'Did you get much sleep?'

'Not much.' Cal was a long way ahead of me. Washed, dressed, but he didn't look as if he'd slept much, either. 'You?'

'I'll survive. And if you're going home today...' He let it lie. A question rather than a statement, as if hoping I might have changed my mind. The temptation to just lie back against the pillows, forget about my nightmare trip to Maybridge and invite him—with my full and wholehearted co-operation—to help himself to my virtue, was very powerful. This was not a day I was looking forward to, but afterwards...well, that was different.

'I'm going,' I said, and wriggled upright, taking a sip of tea. No sugar. I really, really needed sugar... 'I don't suppose I'll be very popular banging up Sophie at the crack of dawn.

'Hardly the crack. It's nearly eleven...'

'What?'

I abandoned the tea, flinging back the covers, swinging my legs over the edge of the bed. 'Why didn't you call me earlier? It'll be dark before I get to Maybridge at this rate!'

'No, it won't. I've spoken to Tessa. She's offered me her car. I'm taking you home.'

'But—'

'Humour me, Philly. Just because you've decided that Don's your man, that you're going back to him, doesn't mean I can just turn off my feelings. I can't stop caring about you, worrying about you.'

I heard the words. Reran them through my head like a tape recording. They still didn't make sense. 'Say that again.'

'I understand, okay? I think you're wrong. I think any man who would let you just walk away after so many years is a fool and that he doesn't deserve you, but—'

'Cal—'

'In fact it occurs to me that I'm an even bigger fool to let you go without fighting for you every inch of the way. The difference between us is that I know you have to make your own decision. Torn, you can never be happy. And I want you to be happy more—'

'Cal—'

'More than I care about being happy myself,' he persisted, as if once he'd stopped he'd never be able to start again. 'I know what you're going to say. It's impossible. Love at first sight doesn't exist. It's lust, sexual attraction…'

'Cal, please—'

'But if it was just that, last night would have been very different. It's crazy. I know it's crazy. We met a couple of days ago. One minute you were this angry young woman berating me for taking her taxi and the next covered with confusion, blushing with embarrassment like a virgin and I wanted to kiss you right there, on the pavement.' He shrugged, finally pausing to let me get a word in, but, hey, I was human, I wanted to hear all of this. 'Actually I wanted to do rather more than kiss you and when you told me where you were going I thought, This is it. Fate. Kismet—'

Okay. That was as good as it got. I wasn't going to be greedy. 'Cal, shut up.'

'Sorry, you don't want to hear that. I didn't mean to lay all that on you. You're lonely and unhappy and you very nearly made the biggest mistake of your life and I understand. Truly.'

'Cal, listen to me. Listen to me very carefully. I'm going home today to tell Don that I've met someone else. Someone who lights up my life like…like the Millennium fireworks. Someone who makes me feel like a real woman—'

'But—'

'Shh!'

'No—'

'Listen,' I said. 'Listen to me.' He battled for a moment with an almost explosive need to interrupt. Battled and won and when he was silent I said, 'I'm going to Maybridge today for only one reason. I'm going to tell him that I know I'm taking a risk. That this guy travels, disappears into the wide-blue yonder in horrible scary planes for months at a time and who knows if he'll come back? But whatever happens I have changed just by knowing him. That Philly-and-Don are history.'

'Philly—'

'I haven't finished,' I said. 'I'm going to tell Don that I love him, will always cherish him as a dear friend. But then that's all we've ever been. Friends. Best friends. Loving friends.' I took a deep breath.

'You see, that thing you said about me blushing like a virgin…well…that's because I am. That was my secret.'

There was a moment of silence while Cal absorbed this.

'But…' Then, 'You mean…'

'I mean that last night was the closest I've ever come to…' And at that point my nerve failed me in the face of his blank astonishment and I stuttered to a halt.

'Making love.' He reached for my hand. Held it. 'Making love,' he said, and then he put his arms around me and pulled me close and I could feel him shaking. 'Last night, in the restaurant, I looked at you and you were so far away and I tried to call you back to me, but you said—'

'I said that I had to go home. To see Don. I had to end that before we could begin.'

'I thought… I thought I was going to die,' he said. 'My heart was breaking and I had to keep acting as if the world hadn't just ended. But I thought I was going to die.'

I lifted my hand to his face, cradling his cheek. 'You said nothing. Didn't try to change my mind.'

'Everyone has to make their own choice, Philly. And even if I'd talked you into bed, what would I have gained?'

'We might both have had a decent night's sleep.' Then I blushed again, because that clearly wasn't what he'd had in mind. 'It's to your credit that you didn't try. You're a true hero, a "parfit gentil knyght".'

'Not that "parfit".' He pushed his fingers into my hair, combing it back from my face. 'It's confession time. You did drop your key on the rug. I stood on it and picked it up while you were searching the cloakroom.'

Yes! Then, 'Can I ask why?'

'Maybe...just for a moment there...I thought I might try it the other way. Are you angry?'

'Angry? Because you wanted me that much? You've got to be kidding.' I was grinning so broadly that there was no point in pretending. 'I'm a bit relieved, to be honest. A hero has to have some flaws, a little grit to make him...a hero.'

'If you don't get out of here right now and get some clothes on—something that covers you from head to toe—I'm telling you, Miss Sensible, Miss Perfect, Miss Anything-But-Dull, that it won't be a little bit of grit, it'll be a damn great—'

I kissed him then, because I couldn't help myself, because I couldn't believe how lucky I was, just *because...*

'Rock,' he groaned, when I paused to catch my breath.

'Yeah,' I said softly. 'I noticed.'

'Out! Now!' I scooped up the very little black dress, along with my shoes and underwear, and fled, but laughing. He caught me at the door and I turned, clutching my clothes to me as he put his hand against it. 'I think you've forgotten something.' And he lifted my coat down from the peg and wrapped it around me. And then he kissed me again as if he couldn't bear to let me go. It was a feeling I understood, shared.

'Cal...'

'I know.' And since he couldn't bear to let me go, he came with me, putting my key in the lock, opening the door for me. 'How long will you be?'

'Give me twenty minutes—' I turned, distracted by a burst of laughter from the kitchen. And then Sophie appeared in the kitchen doorway, coming to a sudden halt as she saw me.

'Philly! Where on earth have you been?' Then she saw Cal and her face clouded. 'You've got a visitor.' And she stepped aside so that I could see Don, behind her.

'Hi, Phil.' He glanced at Cal and then at me with my dress, shoes, underwear in my hands and, well, no matter how innocent our sleeping arrangements had been, how well we'd behaved in the face of all temptation, it was clearly pointless saying so because there wasn't a soul alive who would believe us. And as Don advanced towards us I moved quickly between him and Cal. But he wasn't intent on violence, just on offering his hand. 'I'm Don Cooper,' he said.

Sophie glowered at me. 'Remember him?' she snapped at me. 'The boy back home. The one you said you were going to marry?' Actually, I hadn't said that. Kate had. And she'd been guessing. And just a touch sarcastic. 'Last night I thought *he* was your boy next door.' And she turned her glare on Cal as if her mistake were somehow his fault.

'She's moved,' Cal told her. 'I live next door now.' And he stepped out from behind me and looked Don squarely in the face. 'She's going to marry me.'

Sophie looked confused. That was okay. I wasn't exactly straight on a few points here. Marriage? Who'd said anything about marriage? Don, though, never wavered. 'Good decision,' he said. Then, 'She's the best mate a man could have.' Don's hand didn't waver and Cal finally took it. 'Just don't ever hurt her, or you'll have to answer to me.'

'We were coming to see you today,' I said, cutting in. 'To tell you.'

'I've saved you a wasted trip, then. I just wanted you to know that I'm moving on, Philly. I've met someone, too. A few months back. I was doing his accounts—'

'His?'

'Alex. His name's Alex.'

'Oh.' Then, 'Oh!'

'He runs a garage, classic cars, restorations.' He shrugged. 'He's been trying to get me to join him for months, go into partnership with him.' He looked at me. 'It's not just a business partnership. We're partners in every sense of the word. You do understand?'

I understood. It was like a light bulb going on inside my head. How on earth could I have been so blind? 'I wish you'd told me, Don. I would have supported you.'

'I tried…I really tried to be the son my mother

wanted me to be. Joining the family firm. Settling down with some nice girl. Providing her with grand-children. The fact that she hated you—you were far too strong to meet with her specification for the per-fect daughter-in-law, you know—made it easier to put it off. Just go on the way we were…'

What could I say? That it was my fault for not being more demanding? More of a tiger?

'I really thought that if I concentrated, I could make it with you. Maybe. One day. But then you left and I suppose I came to my senses. Finally asked myself what on earth I thought I was doing. Living a lie. Pretending. I realised just how wrong that was. That you deserve a lot more than I could ever give you. That I deserve a lot more than I was settling for. You do see?'

Oh, yes, I saw. Finally. It was as if I'd been trying to fit a square peg into a round hole; I'd been pushing and twisting and turning it, forcing it to fit. Now it did. Don had repressed everything he was to keep his mother happy. The longing to work with his hands rather than his head. His sexuality. Everything that he was. And I'd made it so easy for him. Too easy…

'I'm sorry, Philly.'

'No, I'm sorry.' And I passed my clothes to Cal and put my arms around Don, held him for a moment. 'Just be happy,' I said. 'Be yourself.' He looked at me and I nodded and it was as if a weight had fallen from his shoulders.

'I have to go. Alex is waiting for me. I'll let you

have our new address. Maybe you'll invite us to the wedding.' And he glanced at Cal.

'You've got it,' he said.

'Which way are you going? Can you give me a lift?' Sophie asked as he headed for the door. 'I promised I'd meet Tony for lunch and I'm going to be late…'

In the silence that rushed back as they left the flat I said, 'Well, that explains one or two things.'

'You had no idea? Even if he wasn't head over heels, most men would have wanted to do a little more than hold hands.'

'He said we should wait. When I was younger I thought it was romantic. And we both lived at home. It's not easy to be alone.'

'It is if you want it enough.'

'Not if you've got a mother like Don's.' Then, 'Well, I'd better go and take a shower,' I said, suddenly embarrassed by my own stupidity. 'Get dressed.'

'Don't go.' He reached out, took my hand. 'Not before I tell you that I was serious when I said it's my intention to marry you.'

I hadn't doubted that he'd been serious when he'd said it. He was not a man to do anything without serious thought. Even so… 'It's a little soon to be thinking of marriage, don't you think?'

'I wasn't suggesting we set a date. I was simply laying down my marker. But you're right, we're going to have to spend a lot of time together. It's a pity you won't fly, or I'd ask you to give up high finance

and take on the job as my very personal assistant on
a tropical island. I can't promise paradise, but if
you're with me it won't be far short.'

I thought about how much I hated flying. The noise
of the engines. The acceleration. The sickening feeling as you left the ground. And realised that to be
with Cal I'd walk through fire. 'It's just possible,' I
said, 'if you were to hold my hand, never let it go, I
might be able to handle the flying.'

'You have my word. We could start with somewhere not too far and work up to long haul. A weekend in Paris, perhaps? Christmas shopping? We could
buy something special for Great Aunt-Alice.'

Oh, help! 'It's not just the flying. The spiders will
be bigger, won't they? A lot bigger? On a tropical
island?'

'Possibly. But I promise you, my love, you'll never
have to put on a brave face again.'

'Just scream if I see one in the bath and you'll be
right there, huh?'

'I don't see any point in frightening the spiders.
We'll share the bath.' And that tell-tale line at the
corner of his mouth presaged a smile. 'That way
you'll never have to scream again.'

At that point I decided that the downside of a few
eight-legged beasties was more than compensated for
by the prospect of sharing my life with Callum
McBride. 'Um, good plan.'

'Pity about all those clothes you bought, though.
Maybe you'd rather spend the next six months com-

muting on the underground to the City—just to get some wear out of them.'

'When are you planning on leaving for paradise?'

'Not for a couple of months.'

'Well, that's all right. I'll take half of them back. Trade them in for a bikini or three.'

He grinned. 'Now that's what I call a *really* good plan.' He reached for me, intent on showing me just how good a plan he thought it was.

'I have to shower,' I said, holding him off. 'And I'm not the only one with messy details to clear up. You have to go and see your parents, Cal.'

'I will. Later. But I'm not going empty-handed. It's nearly Christmas and you're my gift to them.'

'Me?'

'The only thing I can give my father that will atone for my desertion is the possibility of a grandson. A new generation of McBrides.'

'Now you're really getting way ahead of yourself.'

'Way ahead,' he agreed. 'But I think we should put in some serious practice. Starting right now. If I have your full and wholehearted co-operation?'

Absolutely. One hundred per cent. I didn't waste breath telling him. Instead I concentrated on showing him exactly how wholehearted I felt about the future.

Everyone came home for the wedding. It was Christmas again. A year in which I'd learned all the joys of love and of travel. Okay, I still didn't like flying, but Cal held my hand and it was getting better.

I was never going to be completely cured, of course. I liked Cal holding my hand too much.

But now the world was white with frost, the bells were clear and true and the world was lit up with fairy lights, just for us.

My brothers diverted Cal with slanderous stories of my childhood. My sister organised a hen-party to rival her own. My mother looked unbearably smug, as if she'd planned it all. Maybe she had. Well, the part where she'd chiselled me away from my old life, anyway. And she was the one who'd bought that magazine with that quiz blazoned across the cover.

My father took my arm as we stood together in the doorway of the old church and looked down at me. 'Happy?' he asked.

'Blissful,' I said, and then the organ began to play and we moved forward. Standing, waiting for me, his green eyes blazing, afire with love, was Cal, my dearest heart, waiting to promise me the rest of his life. Not paradise. That would be like a hero without a little grit. Too much to live up to.

But close. Very close.

And as I reached him, placed my hand in his, he grasped it firmly in his own and I knew his promise was true and that he would never let it go.

Modern Romance™
...seduction and
passion guaranteed

Tender Romance™
...love affairs that
last a lifetime

Sensual Romance™
...sassy, sexy and
seductive

Blaze
...sultry days and
steamy nights

Medical Romance™
...medical drama on
the pulse

Historical Romance™
...rich, vivid and
passionate

27 new titles every month.

*With all kinds of Romance for
every kind of mood...*

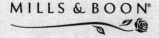

MILLS & BOON

CHRISTMAS
SECRETS

Three Festive Romances

CAROLE MORTIMER   CATHERINE SPENCER
DIANA HAMILTON

Available from 15th November 2002

Available at most branches of WH Smith,
Tesco, Martins, Borders, Eason, Sainsbury's
and all good paperback bookshops.

1202/59/MB50

Don't miss *Book Five* of this BRAND-NEW 12 book collection 'Bachelor Auction'.

Who says money can't buy love?

On sale 3rd January

BA/RTL/5

FREE

2 BOOKS
AND A SURPRISE GIFT!

We would like to take this opportunity to thank you for reading this Mills & Boon® book by offering you the chance to take TWO more specially selected titles from the Tender Romance™ series absolutely FREE! We're also making this offer to introduce you to the benefits of the Reader Service™—

★ FREE home delivery   ★ FREE gifts and competitions
★ FREE monthly Newsletter   ★ Exclusive Reader Service discount
★ Books available before they're in the shops

Accepting these FREE books and gift places you under no obligation to buy; you may cancel at any time, even after receiving your free shipment. Simply complete your details below and return the entire page to the address below. *You don't even need a stamp!*

YES! Please send me 2 free Tender Romance books and a surprise gift. I understand that unless you hear from me, I will receive 4 superb new titles every month for just £2.5? each, postage and packing free. I am under no obligation to purchase any books and may cancel my subscription at any time. The free books and gift will be mine to keep in any case.

N2ZEC

Ms/Mrs/Miss/Mr ....Initials ....
BLOCK CAPITALS PLEASE
Surname ....
Address ....

....

....Postcode ....

Send this whole page to:
UK: FREEPOST CN81, Croydon, CR9 3WZ
EIRE: PO Box 4546, Kilcock, County Kildare (stamp required)

Offer valid in UK and Eire only and not available to current Reader Service subscribers to this series. We reserve the right to refuse an application and applicants must be aged 18 years or over. Only one application per household. Terms and prices subject to change without notice. Offer expires 31st March 2003. As a result of this application, you may receive offers from Harlequin Mills & Boon and other carefully selected companies. If you would prefer not to share in this opportunity please write to The Data Manager at the address above.

Mills & Boon® is a registered trademark owned by Harlequin Mills & Boon Limited.
Tender Romance™ is being used as a trademark.